Caught in the Crossfire

9/14

Caught in the Crossfire

by

Juliann Rich

2014

CAUGHT IN THE CROSSFIRE

ISBN 13: 978-1-62639-070-6

This Trade Paperback Original Is Published By
Bold Strokes Books, Inc.
P.O. Box 249
Valley Falls, NY 12185

First Edition: June 2014

Credits
Editors: Lynda Sandoval and Ruth Sternglantz
Production Design: Susan Ramundo
Cover Design By Sheri (graphicartist2020@hotmail.com)

Acknowledgments

I've always dreamed of writing a book, but it took Jonathan Cooper's story for me to attempt the path toward publication. Thankfully, I haven't had to walk that road alone.

Len Barot and all the hardworking folks at Bold Strokes Books. You've believed in *Caught in the Crossfire* and guided me every step of the way.

Lynda Sandoval and Ruth Sternglantz, my editors. You've helped me take *Caught in the Crossfire* to its highest potential and made the journey a blast to travel.

Saritza Hernández, my super agent. You've set the salsa beat as we've walked this path together and made this long road seem much shorter.

My awesome teachers at The Loft Literary Center: Megan Atwood, Swati Avasthi, Mary Carroll Moore, and Kurtis Scaletta. You've taught by example and made me a better writer.

Ben Barnhart, my mentor. You've equipped me with the tools and confidence to venture into this crazy world.

Aren Sabers, my critique partner. You've given countless hours to *Caught in the Crossfire* and profoundly shaped the book it is today.

Heather Anastasiu, Char Myers, Siobhann Paulman, Judy Steele, Kathryn Swan Kummer, and Maggie Wimberley, my writing buds. You've spoiled me with the gift of thoughtful, honest critique.

The fine folk at Mn Kidlit. You've taught me something every time I've gotten together with you (and not just about where to find the best brew in the Twin Cities!). It is an honor to be a part of your group.

The world's best beta readers: Beverly DeVille, Ruthie Hardin, Ryan Hemauer, Angela McLain, Nicole McLaren, Sue Morrison, and Sharmaine Rich. You've shared your time and valuable reader reactions.

Jeff, my husband extraordinaire. You've been my rock. Matthias, my beautiful son. You've been my hero. My incredible mom. You've been my first and best teacher. What I know of a compassionate and living faith, I learned from you and Dad.

Thank you all.

Dedication

For my son, Matthias, who inspires every word I write.

CHAPTER ONE

Sweat seeped through the thin fabric of my camo T-shirt as I stood on the beach of Spirit Lake, trying to decide the rest of my life. At least, the next thirty days of it. The bulletin board, with the twenty or so flyers that fluttered in the wind, almost convinced me I had any real choice at all.

Outdoor Recreation with Sean promised to teach compass reading and kayaking, but I didn't need a compass to tell me I was lost. Pass.

Healing through Nature with Dawn. To a self-professed science geek, this one had potential. A definite maybe.

Sculpture with Simon. Bingo! Choice number one. I chewed my lip and looked at the other flyers when a familiar voice startled me.

"So, Jonathan! You gonna get your hands dirty with Outdoor Rec this summer, or are you gonna play dress up again with that theater chick? The one with red hair and a funky piercing?" The voice belonged to Jake Miller, the undisputed bane of my summer-camp existence. He sauntered up to me, his black eyes flashing under his greasy bangs. *Here we go again. Same song, seventh summer*. Jake's large hand smacked me on the back, sending me crashing into the bulletin board. I winced and stared into the flyer with a graphic of theater masks.

"G'head. Sign up for Outdoor Rec. All the hot chicks are in Curtain Call." I cocked my head and arched an eyebrow. Just one of the expressions I've perfected over the years. This one says, *I'm into hot chicks.*

"Jesus, Jonathan. That's so gay!"

Nearby a new kid with bright red hair jerked his head out of a book and glared at Jake. "What's that supposed to mean?" He wiped the sweat from his forehead with a rainbow-colored wristband and took a step toward Jake.

"What? What are you talking about?" Jake was caught off guard.

Me too, but for a different reason.

"I said, what's that supposed to mean? That's so *funny*? That's so *great*?" The redheaded boy stood about five inches shorter than Jake. Somehow he seemed taller. He took another step closer, jutting his chin forward. "Tell me that's what you meant when you said *that's so gay.*"

"What's your problem? It's just something people say." Jake threw his shoulders back.

"Something ignorant people say." He clenched his fists. A faint yellow bruise rimmed his left eye.

"Are you calling me ignorant?" Jake curled his lip in a sneer.

"If you have to ask, I'd say the answer is pretty obvious."

"You little prick!" Jake placed his hands on the new kid's chest and shoved. Hard. The redheaded boy stumbled but came back swinging. Nearby, someone gasped and yelled for Paul, the camp director, who stood beside counselors Simon and Dawn over at the registration table.

I once read in *Popular Science* that the human brain can sustain damage when exposed to temperatures of 106 degrees, which was exactly the temperature down on the beach. It must have been, because no one with functioning gray matter would have stepped between those two—and yet, I did. Cringing, brain cell after brain cell frying by the minute, I waited for the impact of a fist…or two.

I got a good look at the new kid while my frontal lobe turned to mush. He leaned closer, not toward me but toward the fight. So close I could have counted his freckles. So close I read the anger in his green eyes. I shuddered at the sheer force of him. He noticed and blinked. Took a step back. His eyes widened and focused on me for the first time since the whole stupid drama began. I felt his gaze slide over my body. His face revealed nothing but his fists relaxed. My skin tingled. Hell, even the hair on my arms stood up as electricity arced between us.

"Gentlemen, that is enough." Paul started toward us with a look that meant there was going to be hell to pay for someone. Out of the corner of my eye I saw two things simultaneously: a blur of red hair moving away and my mother looking up at me from the registration line.

"Cretin!" The new kid hurled the insult at Jake, but I heard it.

"What did you call me?" Jake scowled at the retreating boy who shot a smirk in my direction.

"What was that about?" Paul walked up to us. Behind him, Simon wheeled his chair like a madman to keep up. Trapped behind the registration table by a long line of parents with questions, Dawn frowned in our direction.

"Nothing really. It was just a misunderstanding."

"Just a misunderstanding?" Paul's voice forced me to look at him. The lines around his warm brown eyes had deepened over the past year. "Jonathan Cooper, how long have I known you?"

"Seven years."

"What was that really about?"

I couldn't look at him. Instead, I fixed my eyes on a pile of dried leaves that swirled like a mini tornado in the breeze for a second before they fell back to the ground. Lifeless.

"Nothing." The lie was flimsy, and Paul knew it.

"I see." Paul folded his arms across his chest and frowned. "Just so there aren't any more misunderstandings. At Spirit Lake Bible Camp we follow Christ's example of loving one another. That means no profanity and no fighting. Is that understood?"

"Yes, Paul. Absolutely." Jake let me come up with all the answers. Typical.

"Jonathan! Jake! How the heck have you two been?" Simon rolled his chair between Paul and me, panting.

"Hey, Simon. Good, I guess." I smiled.

"I see you guys met our new camper, Ian McGuire."

"Yeah, what's his problem?" Jake shot a dirty look across the congested campground toward the redheaded boy who sulked next to a middle-aged woman in a denim shirt and a pair of mom jeans.

"Do you remember your first year here when you didn't know anyone?" Simon asked.

"Yeah." Jake stared at his shoes. I nodded.

"I know I can count on both of you to make him feel welcome. I'd better get back to the registration table to help Dawn before she sics her mutt on me." Simon smiled.

"Dawn got a dog?" I looked toward the registration table again and saw a mountain of white fur rolling around on the grass next to Dawn and laughed. "Sorry, Simon, but he doesn't look very threatening."

"You try being within reach of that tongue all the time!" Simon grimaced and wheeled off toward Dawn and her menacing dog.

"Morning, Linda!" Paul smiled as my mom approached. "Looks like registration is almost finished."

Mom nodded. "Just a few people left. How have you been, Paul?"

"Blessed, as always. God is so good." Paul glanced at the counselors who were forming a semicircle in front of the crowd of campers and parents. "I'd better get going. It looks like we're about to start. Good seeing you, Linda, and don't you worry about Jonathan. We'll take good care of him. Jake, why don't we go find your folks? They must be looking for you."

I breathed a sigh of relief as Paul and Jake walked away.

"Who was that boy arguing with Jake? He looks like trouble." My mom glanced toward Ian. She brushed the long hair out of my eyes like I was six and not sixteen. Her tone and gesture said what her words did not. *Stay away from him.*

"I wish I knew, Mom." A shiver ran over my body.

Simon, Dawn, Sara, and the other counselors began to sing, ending any further discussion about Ian McGuire. Male and female voices, equally blended, kicked off opening day at Spirit Lake Bible Camp with a song.

Simon, in his wheelchair, snapped his fingers and sang at the top of his lungs. Beside him Dawn clasped a leash that led to the biggest dog I'd ever seen. Sara—who did indeed have long red hair and a funky piercing not to mention a penchant for glitter eyeliner—winked at me. The song entered the chorus. Simon popped his signature wheelie and danced, to everyone's delight and applause.

"I hope I'm in Simon's cabin again this year."

"Sorry, Jon." My mom looked at the paper she'd gotten from registration. "Looks like you're in the Loon's Nest with a new counselor. His name is Aaron. I think that's him."

Mom pointed at a guy around twenty years old in torn jeans and a tie-dyed shirt, playing a guitar. His light brown curls hung into his eyes, and a silver cross earring dangled from his left ear.

I walked away from Mom toward the counselors until I stood just a few feet away from the guitarist whose hand flew around the neck, expertly landing each chord. His fingers and pick assaulted the strings until they wailed one final note and fell into silent submission. A wooden pendant hung around his neck on a leather cord: God rocks! My name is Aaron.

Hello, Aaron! My heart pounded in the silence.

Stepping forward, Paul offered his usual greeting. "Let us open this summer session by giving praise to the One who has brought us together." Paul bent his head. The sun beat down on his bald spot, bigger than last summer, which gleamed red as the burn set in. His broad shoulders were permanently curved forward. Paul and prayer were close friends.

A few minutes later Mom and I stood on the beach under the weeping willow, breathing in air that tasted bittersweet, and said our good-byes. The sky stretched like a canvas of blue, punctuated only by the throbbing sun. Light danced off the cheerful waves that shimmied along the surface of Spirit Lake.

"I'm going to miss you, Mom."

"Liar!" She laughed. "You're going to have a wonderful month, which is exactly what I want for you."

A gentle breeze rustled her long dark brown hair. Her cheeks flushed, and the muscles of her face relaxed just a bit. She closed her eyes. I knew her mind had traveled far away, across Spirit Lake, over the forest, to a different continent. I raised my camera and zoomed in on her face. The click interrupted her thoughts. She glanced at her watch.

"Oh my, it's nearly fourteen hundred hours." In a military family you keep things: time, schedules, your word. Twenty-four hours a day. With no exceptions.

Take care of your mother while I'm gone, Jon. I'm counting on you.

I will, Dad. I promise.

"He's going to be okay, Mom," I told us both.

"Of course he will. Oh, I almost forgot. Your tokens for the canteen. Will thirty be enough?"

"Yeah, that'll be fine." I slipped the gold tokens into my pocket.

"Okay, then I'd better hit the road. Have fun, Jon. I'll see you in a month."

She walked across the beach, stopping for a moment to turn and blow me a kiss good-bye. I raised a hand and smiled. I imagined her reaching the parking lot, climbing in the car, and navigating the bumpy dirt road. Turning south on Minnesota State Highway 61 and driving toward an empty house. My chest tightened, but then the dazzling blue of Spirit Lake called to me. I ached to plunge into the warm wetness and sink into the silent world. To surface and float, arms outstretched. To feel the sun bake the tension from my body and watch it float away on the rippling waves of good-bye. I kicked off my shoes, let the long blades of grass slip between my toes, and wondered if Iraq had grass. Probably not. Probably couldn't survive in that kind of heat. What could?

I shuddered.

You're going to have a wonderful month, Mom had said. Thirty days of freedom, every one more priceless than a gold coin, stretched before me. I breathed in, slow and steady, and wondered how I'd spend them.

CHAPTER TWO

"All right, rockers!" Aaron's voice boomed as he held a large peace sign above his head. "Follow me to the Loon's Nest." I brushed the sand off my backpack, swung it over my shoulder, and joined the guys who crowded around Aaron. I checked out my cabinmates as we walked across the beach and cringed when I spotted Jake. Aaron led us into the forest and down a dirt path until we reached a fork in the road that was marked by two signs. *Whispering Way, Off Limits to Gentlemen,* pointed to the right and led to the girls' cabins. We turned left, following the sign that read: *Warrior's Way, Run, Ladies, Run!*

"And that, gentlemen, is my number one rule." Aaron grinned. "No making purple allowed. I will be watching."

My head jerked toward Aaron. Making purple? I wondered what he meant as I strolled down the twisting path and listened to the chattering birds that made their home in the forest. Aaron led us past two rustic cabins that held so many memories for me. Two Dancing Bears, Simon's cabin, sported a fresh coat of maroon paint. The Mellow Moose looked bigger with the addition of a deck. Finally, we reached our cabin.

"Welcome to the Loon's Nest." Aaron gestured toward a sign that had an image of a black-and-white loon painted on it. I hung back and waited for the jostling bodies to clear as everyone tried to crowd into the cabin at once. The Loon's Nest smelled of pine trees and boasted the best view of the lake.

"It's every boy's dream vacation spot. Where the mosquitoes are the size of baby pigeons and your fancy smartphones are nothing more than paperweights. No Wi-Fi. Sorry guys." The new campers and the electronically addicted groaned, but I didn't care. Outside, birds chirped. An owl hooted. I spied a top bunk by the window and walked over to claim it. I'd just reached up to put my duffel bag on the mattress when Jake flung his sleeping bag over my head.

"Nice try, Coop, but you know I always call dibs on the top."

"Fine." I sat on the bottom bunk, unzipped my duffel bag, and took out my Bible. I flipped it open and removed the picture I kept there. My father, covered in Kevlar but still so exposed, leaning against a tank and smiling at me. Face blistering from the relentless sun. Sand swirling behind him. Not a care in the world. War suited him.

I slid the picture back into the soft sheets of paper and put my Bible under my pillow for safekeeping.

"Get settled in, guys. We passed the shower room on our way here. You'll find lockers for your hygiene products, so you might want to stop there and stow your stuff. I'm going to go help Paul with a few things. Meet us down at the beach in twenty minutes, okay? We've got something fun planned." Aaron left, the screen door bouncing shut behind him. I untied my sleeping bag and spread it over my bunk.

"Hey, check it out." Jake unzipped his suitcase and took out a huge pile of magazines. "I remembered to pack everything. Well, everything important." Jake opened a magazine and held it up for everyone to see. The centerfold fluttered open. A blond woman with enormous breasts and pink nipples lay across a red sports car. "Play it smart and keep your mouth shut about it to Aaron, and there'll be more where this came from," Jake promised and threatened at the same time. Another one of his signature moves.

I looked. Sure, I looked and immediately wanted to hand the naked woman a shirt to put on. I looked again, hoping to see what the other guys saw, but my stomach cramped. I looked away.

"What's wrong? First time seeing some real tits?" Jake sneered at me.

"Your dad is going to kill you. You do know that, right?"

"Naw. He'd have to admit he has a porn stash before he could give me grief about it, and that's never gonna happen. Maybe you'd like some S and M then." Jake tossed a *Hustler* on my bunk. I glanced at the image on the front cover and threw it back to Jake. I felt like we were back in third grade playing hot potato, except now it was with the tied-up woman with the gag between her teeth.

"Dude, that's so gross." I reached into my duffel bag again and grabbed my insect repellant. I knew from experience that Aaron wasn't kidding about the mosquitoes. I slathered the pungent white cream over my dusty ankles and worked my way up over my thin calves and knees.

"What's wrong with you? You don't like girls? Maybe you'd like a *Playgirl* instead?" I froze at Jake's words. Heads pulled out of their magazines and stared at me. My cheeks burned.

"Why, did you bring your porn stash too?" I recovered. "I wouldn't want to borrow your favorite magazine or anything." Easy laughter broke out in the cabin. Even Jake chuckled. My hands moved again, covering every exposed part of my tanned legs with the cream.

"Okay, choirboy. But if Aaron hears about this from anyone, we'll know who squealed."

"I'd risk getting into trouble if I could make some purple with this babe." Another guy in my cabin laughed, holding up his magazine and leering.

"Hey, what does that mean, make some purple?" I blurted out the words and quickly regretted it. "That's never been a rule here before."

Jake snorted. He looked at me like the word *Loser* blinked on my forehead. "Jeez, Cooper, where have you been living? In a convent?" He snorted again. "Everybody knows that blue equals boys. Pink equals girls. Put one inside the other and what do you get? Purple. Making purple means doing the nasty. You know, the old bump and grind." Jake raised his arms into the air and made two fists with his hands. He thrust his hips forward. I seemed to be the only one who thought that Jake's visual aids were unnecessary. "It's fucking stupid. All this *I'll be watching* stuff is a bunch of bullshit. I bet Aaron's going to use that as an excuse to go out in the woods and get his freak on, if you know what I mean. Which you probably don't."

"Sometimes, Jake, you can be a real ass." I tucked the insect repellant back in my bag, grabbed my sunglasses, and walked out of the cabin. I headed down the path that led back to the main campground and thought of how my father would handle Jake. *Sometimes you charge. Sometimes you retreat. A smart soldier knows when to do which, Jon. That's how wars are won.*

I vowed to keep my distance from Jake.

I couldn't do anything about the fact that he would be snoring and farting above me for the next thirty nights, but the days were mine. Even then, I knew it wouldn't be easy. Camp life was no different from real life, except that everything happened at the lake. All the same rules applied. Some people, like me, slid into the lake. We floated on it and made as few waves as possible. Others lived for the splash—the bigger, the better. Jake, master of the cannonball, always managed to hit a lot of people with just a bit of effort.

Whether I charged or retreated, at some point I knew I was bound to get soaked. "Some wars can't be won, Dad," I said as I walked past the Mellow Moose and caught a glimpse of someone with bright red hair, standing inside the cabin.

Chapter Three

The heat of the late-afternoon sun beat mercilessly on the beach of Spirit Lake where Aaron had asked us to gather. Paul instructed us to find someone we didn't know to be our partner. I looked around, searching for him.

"Hi, do you want to be my partner?" A pretty girl with long brown hair startled me. I hadn't seen her approaching.

"Um, thanks, but I already have a partner."

"You do?" She looked around, confused.

"Yeah, he's around here somewhere." I squirmed.

"Oh, okay. I'd better find someone else then." She looked disappointed.

"Sorry."

"No problem." She turned and walked away. Jake descended on her like a hawk spotting a field mouse. I almost called her back, but a glimpse of red on the far side of the beach caught my attention. I wove through the sea of bodies until I stood next to him.

"Hey, um, wanna be my partner?" I asked. So lame.

He frowned. "Technically, we have met, but I guess I don't really know you. Why do you want to be my partner?"

"Um, I don't know." My mouth was so dry I could have drunk Spirit Lake, fish and all. "I guess I just thought, you know, you're new here."

"Obviously. So you thought you'd offer to be my partner?"

"Yeah."

"Whatever."

"I'm Jonathan Cooper." I stuck my hand out like a dork. He smirked, and I jammed it into my pocket.

"Ian McGuire. Hey, about earlier—"

"Listen up, everyone!" Paul called out. "Once you've found your partner, sit down on the ground. When everyone is seated, we'll have some fun."

We sat on the sandy beach and waited, uncertain what fun he had planned for us.

"Earlier?" I shifted positions. My knee brushed up against his leg.

"Yeah, with the cretin."

"Oh, that. No sweat." Except that there was. Lots of it, as a matter of fact.

"I wasn't thanking you. Do you have an ego or what? I wanted to tell you that I can take care of myself. Next time, remember that." I didn't know how to field that kind of honesty, so I just sat there, slack-jawed, and stared at him.

"You have five minutes each to pantomime three things about yourself," Paul said. "You may get up and move around if you need to, but there is no talking. Afterward you'll introduce one another, and we'll see if your partner correctly figured out the three things about you. This should be fun! Remember, no talking. No whispering. No mouthing words. No making sound at all. No props. Ready? Begin!" Paul blew the whistle.

The beach suddenly became an oven. I looked across at Ian. He shook his head and pointed at me. I pointed back, but he crossed his arms in front of his body. I tried to remember the stage directions from a one-act play I'd been in the previous year. I stood up, swung my arms in the air dramatically, pulled my hands to my heart, fell to one knee, and hung my head. It had been a tragedy, but from the look on Ian's face, he was watching high comedy. I stood again and walked forward, bowing deeply while he clapped without making a sound.

Bravo. He mouthed the word.

My stomach fluttered, and subconsciously my hand reached for the cross necklace, a gift from my mother. “No props, Jonathan!” Nathan, the junior counselor, shouted at me. I tucked the cross back under my T-shirt.

I kicked a pretend soccer ball around. Dodged and ducked. Even headed it off my forehead. Aiming, I kicked it square into the pretend net and then did a lame little dance in celebration. Ian yawned.

Finally I cupped my left hand in front of my face and adjusted an imaginary camera with my right hand. Peering through the nonexistent lens, I pretended to focus on Ian who mouthed the word *cheese* through a stupid fake grin. I pushed my right index finger down and pretended to take a picture. Just then the willow tree behind him glowed in the golden sunlight. I squinted through the imaginary lens and regretted leaving my real camera back at the cabin. I lay down underneath the willow tree and took another pretend picture of it, not giving a damn how weird I might look. Nothing mattered but seeing every detail of the sun-bathed branches and the patches of blue sky that framed the picture in my mind.

Paul blew the first five-minute whistle. I sat up and saw Ian beaming at me. I looked away, hoping he hadn’t noticed the flush of red I could feel creeping over my face.

“Your turn.” I dared to look at Ian whose smile had changed to a frown. He reached behind him and produced a small notebook. It was folded in half and tattered from being shoved in his back pocket. He opened it and began to write. *No props!* I mouthed, which didn’t break the rules in my opinion, though Simon pointed a finger at me and shook his head. I pointed at Ian.

“No props, Ian!” Simon chided him.

Ian shrugged his response, put the journal away, and shot a dirty look in my direction. *Narc,* he mouthed.

He stood up, rigid. He stepped forward and swung his right foot out in a small arc and then snapped it back until his heels tapped. His right arm snapped into a ninety-degree angle with his body. Then his hand snapped up into a forty-five-degree arc until the tips of his fingers hovered just above his right eyebrow. His hand, fingers together but outstretched, shielded his eyes from the sun. Every move precise. Every angle perfect. The expression drained from Ian's face except for his eyes. They stared into mine like two lasers, the one discrepancy.

Shoulders back. Arm higher, Jon. Hold that hand steady. Never connect eyes.

The nearly perfect military salute. I could have identified it from my high chair.

Tears burned my eyes. My vision blurred. My heart tripped in my chest.

The thin wall that separated my worlds collapsed, and suddenly the sandy beach burned hot. Iraq hot. The wind swirled around us and tasted of spices I couldn't and didn't want to name. Someone, maybe Jake, shouted. I jumped and looked around.

It was just the beach at Spirit Lake Bible Camp. I forced my breathing to slow. My head spun. I blinked twice and focused on Ian who waited at attention. The little toy soldier, ready for war.

His shoulders were squared. His fingertips did not quiver.

At ease, I mouthed. Ian's arm fell to his side. Emotion flooded his face, like a flickering flame that had been relit.

Paul blew the whistle again, signaling the end of Silent Introductions, Part 1. Part 2 loomed. I made Ian go first when it was our turn to introduce each other. I expected some push back, but he surprised me.

He stood up and cleared his throat. "I'd like to introduce you to Jonathan Cooper. Jonathan is a veteran at Spirit Lake Bible Camp. He's been coming here since he was a kid."

How did he know that?

"In fact, he's hoping to be a junior counselor here next summer. Paul, I'd seriously consider giving him the position. He deserves it." Ian was the actor now. He had the whole camp eating out of the palm of his hand. "However, you may want to consider a few of his drawbacks. For one, he doesn't know how to tie his shoes. He tries real hard though. In fact, he knelt over and looked at his feet for a good ten seconds, but nope. Couldn't figure it out. He also has narcolepsy and might need to lie down unexpectedly, preferably under the shade of a nice tree."

I wanted to be swallowed up by the beach.

"Jonathan also has a raging case of athlete's foot. Either that or he plays soccer. Honestly, I couldn't tell which. Obviously making Jonathan Cooper a junior counselor is a big gamble, but I'd give him high points for being a good sport, wouldn't you?" Ian bowed and the traitors clapped.

Paul laughed so hard tears actually ran down his cheeks. Even Simon chuckled. I looked over at the brown-haired girl, the one I should have chosen as a partner. Her eyes said she understood. At least she wasn't laughing at me. Next to her sat Jake, wolf whistling at the top of his lungs. One look at him told me I could look forward to plenty of foot jokes over the next four weeks. At least he wouldn't know what narcolepsy meant. Ian bowed again and sat down.

"Hi, everyone! First, let me make something clear. I play soccer. I do not have athlete's foot." I stood up, lifted my right foot to feign a kick, and almost died of embarrassment when my shoelaces swung out in the air.

"My partner is Ian McGuire." Something in my words struck me as odd, but I couldn't take them back. "As you can tell, he's smart, funny, and exactly the leprechaun we've needed at Spirit Lake Bible Camp. Ian, where did you stash your pot of gold?" Okay, not the most brilliant thing I could have come up with, but I only had fifteen seconds' notice. Ian grinned and pointed toward the forest. "Oh, and he's a writer, I think. He sure is good with words. Don't you agree?" The clapping, I suspected, was still meant for Ian.

I started to say something about the salute, but the words died in my mouth as I realized that it had not been part of Silent Introductions at all. It had been between us, a private McGuire moment.

Finally, I swallowed the last dose of humiliation, sat down on the beach, and listened to the brown-haired girl as she struggled to make Jake sound interesting.

❖

"Hey, how did you know all those things about me?" I grilled Ian as we walked toward the dining hall. The scent of barbecued beef and corn on the cob filled the air. "That I've been coming here for years and that I want to be a junior counselor next year?"

"It's obvious, isn't it?" The color of Ian's eyes, I decided, was smug. Not green. Smug.

"Not to me, it isn't. Do you read people's minds or something?"

"Maybe."

I looked at him curiously. I mean the guy knew some seriously uncanny stuff about me.

He saw my gullible face and laughed. "Okay, not really. The first time I met you, you jumped in between me and Jerk."

"You mean Jake."

"No, I meant Jerk. Don't interrupt."

I laughed, despite myself.

"Conclusion: you're willing to go out on a limb for someone you don't know. Sounds like someone who wants to be a junior counselor to me."

"True, I guess. And the fact that I've been coming here since I was a kid?"

"Easy. I overheard you tell Paul you'd known him for seven years."

"Oh yeah, I guess I did." It all made perfect sense when he explained it. "Still, the junior counselor thing was pretty slick."

"Basic observation and conclusion. It's not rocket science."

"But what was up with the salute?"

"You're a military kid, right? C'mon, Jonathan. It's written all over you."

"Yeah, I am. I just didn't know it was obvious."

"It is. At least to me." Ian frowned.

"Man, you nailed that salute. It was perfect. But you were supposed to be doing something about yourself. Not me. So technically you cheated."

"I won't tell if you won't." He slid into his place in the dinner line. Eyes still locked on mine, his hand reached for a tray and silverware.

"C'mon, Ian. Someone taught you that. Are you a military kid too?"

"I'm nobody's kid." The silverware clattered onto the plastic tray.

His eyes said *drop it.* So I did as he walked away and sat at a table by himself.

The salute, just like Ian, remained a mystery.

Chapter Four

My head spun as I crawled into my sleeping bag. It was hot enough in the cabin to sleep on top of it, but I figured I should make the mosquitoes work for their feast. Improve the species by winnowing out the weak.

WWJD? A hint of moonlight peeked through the window, and I read the letters someone had carved into the wooden base of the upper bunk, directly over my head. *What would Jesus do?* Good question. Most of the time I even came up with a pretty good answer.

"Lord, please watch over my dad. Keep him safe and bring him home to us soon. And please, be with my mom," I whispered.

Jake's obnoxious snores interrupted my prayers. The chirping of crickets filled the night. I'd loved listening to crickets ever since Dawn taught me about them last summer. She said that some male crickets dig tunnels into the ground with amphitheater-shaped openings where they sit, rubbing their wings together to produce the familiar chirping sound. *The cricket song we all hear*, Dawn had explained, *is actually nothing more than an extremely loud booty call that can be heard miles away by female crickets*. She had pointed out that there were three songs: the initial call, the love song when the male senses that the female is nearby, and the celebratory song after they've mated. *Talk about kissing and telling!* she had joked.

Jake's breathing finally quieted into a rhythmic pattern. I closed my eyes and floated on the gentle waves that lapped against the shore of Spirit Lake where thousands, maybe millions of male crickets were burrowed in their amphitheater holes, chirping their songs.

That's a whole lot of horny insects.

Silence filled the cabin as the kiss-and-tell songs of the crickets died away. Aaron slowly unzipped his sleeping bag. I closed my eyes and pretended to be asleep. This scene was not supposed to be witnessed, I was certain. The screen door creaked open, and I heard the muted sound of it carefully being closed. *What are you up to?* My curiosity nibbled at me like a mosquito until I finally swatted it and got out of my bunk. I stood outside the cabin, looking for something to indicate which way Aaron had gone. The sound of a snapping branch came from deep within in the forest. *Gotcha.* I followed the narrow path that led away from camp and deeper into parts of the forest I'd never explored. I walked slowly, carefully, crouching low. Suddenly I ran out of trail and stood at the edge of a clearing, unable to believe or look away from the scene in front of me. Aaron leaned against the trunk of a tall tree, his face turned up toward the sky. Moonlight beat down on him. A smile played across his face. A slight figure with red hair knelt in front of him. Sara? The name exploded in my mind. I stepped into the clearing and walked closer toward Aaron who ran his fingers through the short red hair. *Short* red hair? Ian turned and looked directly at me with those remarkable green eyes and winked.

My heart threatened to pound out of my chest. I flailed and kicked. I tried to sit up and couldn't. The stupid sleeping bag wrapped my whole body in a straitjacket. *Where am I?* I wondered, half-asleep and disoriented. I shook my head, but the vivid image of Aaron and Ian refused to go away.

I looked around the dark cabin and breathed a sigh of relief. *It was just a dream. I'm at camp*. My breathing slowed. I peered through the darkness and spotted Aaron, arm flung over his head, sound asleep on his cot. I lay back down on my bunk, aware of my hard-on.

What would Jesus do? I stared at the carved letters that drilled me in the darkness. I had no answer. *Jesus, please forgive me,* I prayed as I turned my face into my pillow and hid my tears. Even from myself.

CHAPTER FIVE

The first Sunday of camp dawned and threatened to be the clichéd beautiful day with blue skies void of clouds and just the right amount of breeze. I walked down to the beach and joined the rest of the camp for Songs by the Shore. Spirit Lake Bible Camp had no physical church. Just Paul, sitting on the large rock in the shadow of the beautiful hand-carved cross, talking with us as if our thoughts and opinions were the most important thing he could ever hear. It was church the way church was supposed to be.

As I listened to Aaron's guitar music, I prayed. For my father's safety. For my mother's strength. Those were easy prayers. Still shaken from my dream the night before, I decided to get real with God.

Dear Lord, I prayed silently, *please make these feelings and thoughts go away. Protect me from these dreams.*

After church and a huge lunch, I sprawled out on the dock until my skin began to sizzle. The cool water looked too inviting to resist. My head broke the surface, and I saw Ian, leaning against the willow tree and alternating between staring off into space and writing. I walked out of the lake and approached the willow tree. Parting the long branches like a beaded hippie curtain, I ducked inside.

"Hey!" Ian objected as the water, which still clung to my body, dripped on his notebook.

"Sorry. I didn't mean to get your letter wet."

He looked confused for a moment, and then grinned as understanding crossed his face. "Your assumption is erroneous."

"My assumption is what?"

"Erroneous. It means you guessed wrong. This isn't a letter."

"Oh, what are you writing?" I snuck a peek at his notebook, but he closed it before I had a chance to read anything.

"Nothing. Why?"

"I don't know. Just curious."

"Yes, you are. Quite curious." Ian's gaze held mine, and then dropped to the journal in his hands. "I was writing a poem, okay? And now you may commence laughing at me."

"Why would I do that?" I stared at the light that filtered through the green branches and cleared my throat. "Believe me when I say it was an awful day. Such a sad, sad way to start the month of May."

"Stop! Please stop!" He covered his ears and screwed up his face. "You're the worst poet ever!"

I laughed and held up my make-believe camera and took a make-believe photo of him. "Okay, can we be friends if I swear I'm better with a lens?"

He groaned. "Friends, huh? Do you promise to never write another poem?"

"On one condition."

He raised an eyebrow. "Mr. Junior Counselor wannabe, official greeter of all new campers and fight referee, is demanding conditions now?"

"I am," I said, reaching for his journal. "I promise to never write another poem if you let me read yours."

He yanked his notebook away from me and ducked through the willow's branches. "Guess I'll have to get used to listening to crap poetry then," he said as he strode away.

"Okay, but you're going to have to help me think up more words that rhyme with day," I shouted after him.

He swiveled and stared at me. "Off the top of my head…bent to *pray*, over a cafeteria *tray*, heart in dis*may*, you need to break a*way*."

I don't care what he said. Ian McGuire could read minds.

❖

I sat on the beach for a while, my head spinning. Just hours before I had prayed for God to take these feelings from me, and what had I done? Promptly searched out Ian. Heck, I'd even recited poetry to him. Bad poetry. My stomach knotted. My mouth tasted sour and no amount of swallowing made it go away. I stood up and wandered over to the canteen.

"Mr. Cooper!" Sara grinned at me from behind the counter. "What can I get you today?"

"How about a Dr Pepper?"

"Coming right up." Sara poured the soda and handed it to me. "That'll be one canteen token, please."

I reached into my pocket and fished out a gold coin. "Thanks, Sara." I gulped the Dr Pepper, but it didn't wash away the sour taste in my mouth.

"Say, I saw you talking with Ian McGuire. It's great that you're reaching out to him. You know, life has kicked the kid around like a Hacky Sack. He doesn't know it, but he needs a friend. Something tells me you're exactly the person for the job."

"Thanks."

"Any word on your dad yet?" Sara asked, startling me as I realized that she knew. Of course, all the counselors knew. My mom would have made sure of that.

"No, not yet. Soon, I hope." I looked away from Sara and toward the lake. "See you at Curtain Call, okay, Sara?"

"You got it. See you tomorrow morning." She smiled.

I finished my Dr Pepper and waded into the cool lake, step after step. The burning in my flesh eased, at least for now. I held my breath and let my body float on the surface. My hair fanned out around me. I stared into the sun until my pupils shrank and my retinas burned. I closed my eyes. Blinking spots and a throbbing black globe floated across the screen of my closed eyelids. So real at first. Sharply outlined and clearly visible. Then the fading began. Bit by bit until the screen filled with just a warm red glow.

I exhaled and felt Spirit Lake pull me beneath the surface. Water seeped into the sockets of my eyes and filled my nostrils and then I was in…over my head.

❖

Covered in sand and reeking of lake water, I headed for the boys' shower room. I tried to push thoughts of Ian out of my mind as I turned my face into the full stream of hot water, making it impossible to open my mouth or eyes. Even then, I couldn't block out the sounds of the other guys who stood, naked, water splashing against their flesh. They didn't seem to mind the lack of privacy, but I couldn't stand the old-school mass shower room. I envied them.

Eventually I had to surface; it was either that or drown. My head turned slightly for just one moment. I took a deep drag of hot steamy air, wiped the water from my face, and opened my eyes. The bar of soap slipped through my fingers and thudded to the floor. *Don't look. Don't look.* I knelt and retrieved the bar, glistening white against the tile floor. A rolled up towel bit into someone's naked ass with a loud snap. I peeked.

"Hey, no fair!" a confident male voice yelled. No chance of cracking there. Well on his way to manhood, I noticed, as I reached for my shampoo and poured it over my shaggy hair. The scent of musk filled the air around me. My fingers scrubbed and scratched until the lather exploded. It slid down my forehead. *There's no other way,* I tried to convince myself as the stinging soap hit my eyes. But even the tears were not enough to blind me from Ian's slim figure as he strode into the room, proving to everyone he was a true redhead. There were half a dozen open showerheads, but he chose the one next to me and turned it on. Full blast. He stepped into the heat. Steam sizzled, rose from his body, and evaporated in the hot, humid air.

"Aaahh." His hands moved the bar of soap over his body. Across his arms, his chest, his stomach, and below. I breathed in the scent of his soap, burned from the nearness of his body. Still covered in suds, I bolted.

I wrapped my towel securely around my waist, leaned on the sink, and waited for the room to stop spinning. I squeegeed the dripping layer of condensation off the rippled metal mirror with my hand and checked out my distorted reflection. I ran a comb through my long hair and smiled. Better. More like what a junior counselor should look like. Time for a shave.

I ran my fingertips along my cheek and chin. Still not much scruff to speak of, but I picked up the can of shaving lotion anyway and shot a wad of slippery Smurf-blue gel into my hand. I covered my burning cheeks with the cool lather.

The flash of red in my mirror grabbed my attention. Turning, I saw Ian's fully lathered face reflected in his own mirror. He slid a straight razor over his cheek, gathering a blade full of lather.

"Hey, what's that?"

"The only way to shave." He wiped the lather off and proudly held the razor toward me. It was beautiful with its iridescent pearl handle.

"Aren't you afraid you'll cut yourself?" The blade was samurai sharp. I handed it back to Ian.

"Not really. The trick is to shave in the direction your hair grows. Never against it. It's easy once you know what you're doing." He faced the mirror and pressed the blade against his cheek, guiding it around the curve of his chin and down his neck.

Suddenly a toxic cloud wafted off Jake who stood two sinks down from Ian, trying to cover up the smell of DEET with half a can of Axe body spray. You always could count on Jake to make a bad situation worse.

"Cool. Where did you learn to shave like that?"

“My dad taught me.” Ian flinched as a thin ribbon of blood snaked down his neck. “Shit.”

“Hold still.” I tore off the corner of a Kleenex and pressed it against the small cut on his neck. His skin was as soft as my voice. “Poet, mind reader, semiprofessional barber. What other talents do you have?”

“Wouldn’t you like to know?” He laughed as he walked over to his locker and let the towel slip from his waist. “And for the record, I’m fully accomplished with a razor. You distracted me.”

I watched out of the corner of my eye as he stepped into his shorts and pulled a T-shirt over his head. Slipping the razor into his pocket, he walked out the door. I almost called after him to ask if he wanted to meet me for dinner, but I didn’t. My eyes, reflected in the mirror, knew the reason why the words stuck in my throat.

I was afraid he would say no.

I was even more afraid he would say yes.

CHAPTER SIX

So this is Curtain Call's motley crew this summer?" Sara stood on the grassy stage of the outdoor theater on Monday morning and evaluated the group of kids who had shown up for her first theater-club meeting. The air filled with the scent of freshly mowed grass. "Let me see, all I need is a play that casts four girls and two boys? No problem." I looked around our group. Shocked, I saw Ian, sitting apart from the rest of us. His mouth was pinched, like he'd taken a bite out of a lemon and the taste of it lingered.

"Let's begin by going around the circle and telling our names and something unusual about ourselves. My name is Sara Reid. The unusual thing about me is that I never have the same hairstyle for more than six months. I'm thinking of going platinum blond with fuchsia and bright blue streaks next. What do you think?"

I chuckled. Sara's style could put Lady Gaga to shame any day.

"Jonathan, would you go next?"

"Yeah, sure. My name is Jonathan Cooper, but you already know that." I shot Ian a dirty look, pretty sure no one would ever forget my name, thanks to him. Then I got stuck. "Um, I like photography, soccer, and acting. I don't know if that's unusual or not, but I can't think of anything else."

"Jonathan is being modest. He played Jesus last summer in *Godspell*. He had the whole audience in tears." Sara smiled at me. "Next, please."

The introductions didn't take long. There weren't that many of us. Kari: blond and fidgety. She talked at the speed of someone in need of a 12-step program for Red Bull. Cats were her thing and she owned six of them. Definitely unusual. MacKenzie: extremely thin, dark brown hair, and Angelina lips. She rambled on about her theater group back home and all the plays she'd starred in. Yadda, yadda, yadda. I actually caught Sara rolling her eyes. Lily: plain and, well, plump. She stared at the lake and talked in whispers. She didn't have to tell us she was shy. She wanted to help with costumes but begged not to have to act. Smiling, I welcomed her to Curtain Call.

"Okay, hello, my name is Bethany Frasier," the brown-haired girl who had asked me to be her partner during Silent Introductions said. "What's unusual about me? Not much, really. Except that I'm homesick. My mom homeschools my brothers and sisters and me. There are nine of us. Oh, I guess that's unusual. This is the first time I've been away from my family. Four weeks seems like such a long time."

Bethany may have been addressing the whole group, but her eyes didn't leave my face.

"I'm in Sara's cabin and she invited me to Curtain Call. I've never been in a play before, so I hope I'm not too terrible."

"Thank you, Bethany," Sara said. "While you're here, I want you to think of us all as your family away from home. And now, Ian, would you please introduce yourself?"

He frowned as our eyes turned to him. "I'm from Wisconsin. There's not much interesting about me except I don't have a clue what I'm doing here. Sean, my counselor, told me to get my butt over to Curtain Call, so here I am."

"Thanks for coming today. And Ian, I'm quite certain that there are plenty of interesting things about you. Can you think of one?"

Ian shrugged. "Okay, here's one. I refuse to eat at Wendy's. Hamburgers are not supposed to be square. They should be round. I guess that's weird enough to qualify as interesting."

Everyone laughed. I laughed too, but I recognized the sarcasm in his voice.

"It certainly does." Sara chuckled. "Ian, you're here because of your performance the other day at Silent Introductions. Right then and there I knew I had to have you in Curtain Call." She produced a box of doughnuts and passed them to Ian first. "The choice is yours, Ian. Stay, and I promise to bribe you shamelessly with sweets. Today it's doughnuts. By the way, they're round. Just like they're supposed to be." She grinned. "What do you say, Ian? Will you join our cast?"

"Yeah, okay." He chose one and took a huge bite. Custard squirted out and dripped down his chin. I felt my focus glaze over and my resolve turn to jelly.

"Okay, crew, we need to get down to business. *Godspell* is going to be a tough act to follow, but we're up to it." Sara handed a stack of bound scripts to me. I took one and passed them around.

I scanned the title page—*Pass the Pepcid*—and flipped to the list of characters on page two. Herod, Herodias, John the Baptist, Salome, Guests at Dinner, Executioner. "The story of the beheading of John the Baptist?" I guessed.

"Yup. It's one of the bloodiest stories in the Bible. Whenever I think of it, I get a stomachache. It's a modern interpretation. John the Baptist is a news anchor on CESR, the local TV station for Rome. Caesar, get it? Jonathan, would you read King Herod? Ian, I'm seeing you as John the Baptist. I always pictured him as a redhead for some reason. For MacKenzie who loves the dramatic, please read Queen Herodias. Bethany, Salome, the daughter of Herodias. Kari, would you please read the role of Female Dinner Guest, and I'll read the role of Executioner for now. I have an idea for casting that part. Lily, I want you to close your eyes and imagine what you'll need for costuming and sets. Okay, does everyone know what you're doing?"

We nodded.

"I've got a confession to make right now. What you're holding is an original piece. It has never been performed. In fact, no one has ever even read it before." Sara twisted her hands.

"But where did you get it then?" MacKenzie asked.

"I imagine that she wrote it herself." Ian's hand strayed to his notebook.

"That's right, Ian, I did." Sara stared at the script in her hand. "And I haven't had the guts to let anyone read it until now. Be kind."

❖

Before I knew it, we had finished act 1. I tried my best to sound kingly, and I think I did okay. Ian blew me away with his smooth news-anchor voice. Bethany was way too tame. She needed to loosen up. MacKenzie nailed the part of haughty Herodias. Big surprise there. Not. By the end of our first Curtain Call meeting, we were all in agreement: *Pass the Pepcid* was going to be a blast to perform.

"Fantastic job, everyone! I think this is the most talented group I've ever had in Curtain Call," Sara gushed.

No one would hear from me that Sara said that every year, sort of like the judges on *American Idol*. This year though, it seemed like she might mean it.

"Now, besides working on memorization, there's something else I want you to do. It's important for a cast to have chemistry in real life. For the rest of the afternoon, I want you guys to hang out and get to know each other."

"Are you coming with us, Sara?" Lily asked.

"No, I want you to bond just as a cast. Besides, I promised Sean I'd help him prep for his first canoe class. Gotta run—I'm late." Sara headed toward the boathouse.

"What should we do? Does anybody have any ideas?" Bethany asked.

"We could take a pontoon boat out on the lake," I suggested. "That way we could practice our lines without being overheard." Everyone jumped onboard with the plan. The girls went to ask Hannah, Paul's wife and the camp cook, for some afternoon snacks while I stepped onto the beach and walked toward the boathouse.

"Coming?" I called back to Ian who sprinted to catch up with me.

"You know," he said as his footsteps fell into a comfortable rhythm with mine, "you're a natural leader. People listen to your ideas. You'd make a great junior counselor, except..."

"Except what?"

Ahead of us the door to the boathouse opened and Sean and Sara emerged, their arms filled with paddles and life jackets.

"It's just, you know..." He slowed his steps. "These people." He jerked his head toward Sean and Sara. "They don't seem like they'd be okay with someone who is..."

"Who is what?" I frowned at him.

It slipped then, the mask he wore that said he didn't give a damn what anybody thought of him. "Nothing. You're going to be a great junior counselor. Just ignore me. Everyone does."

"But," I blurted out, "I don't want to ignore you. In fact, I'd like to—" The sound of paddles crashing to the ground stopped me from saying anything else, which was perfect because my mouth had evidently disconnected from my brain.

"Gentlemen!" Sean walked up to us. "What trouble are you two getting into today?"

When words failed me, it fell to Ian to plead our case for checking out a pontoon, and I had to hand it to him. In no time at all we were cruising Spirit Lake with me at the helm, the girls at the bow, and Ian brooding in the passenger seat next to me. I opened the engine up full throttle and turned into a wave, causing spray to fly up and hit him. Unfortunately, it also soaked the girls who raised such holy hell I decided to coast to a stop and drop anchor.

"Now what?" Bethany asked. "Do we run lines or something?"

"Naw," Ian said. "Plenty of time for that. Sara wants us to get to know each other. You know what that calls for, right? A game of Truth or Dare."

A good junior counselor would have said no to Ian's ludicrous suggestion. A good junior counselor would have put his foot down, even if it had rocked the pontoon. Hell, a good junior counselor would have jumped overboard and swum for shore when he had the chance. I didn't do any of those things. Instead, I joined the others as they sat in a circle on the deck of the pontoon. The sun beat down on my body, burning up the last bit of common sense God gave me. Must have been 106 degrees again.

"Sure, Truth or Dare sounds like fun." I listened to the water smack against the bottom of the boat, rocking it back and forth, and went with the flow.

"Great. I'll start. Jonathan, Truth or Dare?" Ian grinned wickedly. I should have known. At the very least, I should have suspected.

"Truth." A metallic-blue dragonfly hovered for a moment before it darted away. In the distance I heard the splash of a fish jumping.

"Who was the first person you kissed and what was it like?" Ian raised a can of orange Crush to his lips and winked at me as he took a long sip. The flush started on the back of my neck. Just the word *kiss* coming out of his mouth could do that to me.

The tension in our group hitched up a notch or two as they leaned in, hungry for the scoop. Ready to devour the steamy details. Only…I didn't have any.

"Easy. It was my mom and it was probably sticky. I was a big fan of pudding back then." I grabbed a Dorito, popped it into my mouth, and licked the dusting of seasoning from my fingers.

"No fair!" MacKenzie shouted. "That's not what Ian meant. He meant your first real kiss. With a girl."

"Yeah, well, when that actually happens, I'll let you know." I grinned.

MacKenzie's mouth dropped open. Ian leaned back against the metal railing of the boat. Satisfaction oozed from him.

"You mean you've never been kissed?" MacKenzie looked incredulous. The boat tilted and settled again as the pontoon navigated a wave.

"Nope. Not yet."

"We're definitely going to have to change that." Ian's voice rumbled low with hidden meaning. My eyes darted to his face.

"Okay, Bethany, your turn. Truth or Dare?" Kari laughed, miraculously, gloriously oblivious to Ian's body language.

"Um, dare. Sure, why not?" Bethany looked fearless. The sun brought out the natural streaks of gold in her hair. MacKenzie leaned forward and whispered something into Kari's ear. Giggling and nodding, she shot a knowing look at me and winked.

Holy crap! The voice screamed in my head, the way it does when you're stuck at the top of a roller coaster. Right before it starts to move and suddenly you're plunging. Out of control. Ready to vomit.

"I dare you to kiss Jonathan on the mouth for one minute. What you do with your tongues is up to you," Kari announced.

Bethany turned white and stared at me. Ian sat up fast, blinking. Something inside me balled up and panicked.

"Ready, get set, kiss!" MacKenzie stared at the second hand on her watch. Bethany leaned forward, awkward, fear in her eyes. A cloud crossed in front of the sun, casting Ian's face in shadows.

"Don't worry. It's going to be okay," I whispered to both of us. Her soft lips pressed against the hard ridges of my mouth. We plunged. Racing out of control. Wind rushing past us. My stomach lurched. My scream never escaped because her mouth held me prisoner.

"Thirty seconds! Last chance to move into second base!" MacKenzie yelled.

Bethany groaned or moaned. I couldn't tell which, so I peeked. Her loose shirt hung open as she leaned toward me. Hello! Two full, rounded breasts spilled out of silly pink lace. Her chest heaved, straining the thin fabric. My stomach tightened, and I shifted my eyes away quickly. Though her long brown hair had fallen around us, I saw Ian, eyes smoldering and fists tightened. The boat tossed, flinging Bethany and her breasts toward me, our kiss unbroken. The air filled with the scent of coconut. Rounded, firm coconut. The scent of suntan lotion came up off her skin, the bronzing kind. I reached to steady her.

"And…time!" MacKenzie called. Clapping and whistling echoed across the water as Bethany broke off our kiss. She paused before she pulled away. Her face was flushed; her breath came in quick, hushed gasps. Her dark brown eyes struggled to hold mine.

"That was more than just okay, Jonathan," she whispered into my ear before she sat back down.

The boat swayed. The sun baked. All eyes were on me, but I couldn't talk.

My eyes fixed on the mangled can in Ian's clenched fist and the sticky orange liquid that spilled over his fingers…and I knew.

I wasn't the only one with a crush.

Chapter Seven

"Hey, wait up! I'll join you," Ian called to me as I walked along the beach later that evening, occasionally stopping to pick up and examine a flat, thin stone. Looking for just the right one. "Whatcha doing?"

"Not much. Just skipping rocks." Spirit Lake stretched in front of us. The sound of laughing voices carried over the campground.

"Cool. I've never done that before."

"Really? It's easy. Like this." I leaned back, arm extended, and aimed low so the stone would skim the surface and skip across it. Except it didn't. My first attempt flopped and sank.

"Like that, huh?" Ian mocked.

"Not exactly." I picked up another stone, wafer thin and flat, and let it fly. One…two…three…yes, four full skips and then it too sank and disappeared, but man, it was beautiful while it flew! "More like that." Pride crept into my voice.

"Okay, my turn." Ian crouched and examined the rocks. He took his time. Finally he chose one, elliptical and rounded at the bottom.

"Mmm, I wouldn't—"

He stopped me with one glance.

"Oh, okay. Whatever you want." I grinned.

Ian wound his arm back like a baseball player and pitched the rock. The splash was even bigger than I'd hoped.

"Excellent form, McGuire. You might have broken a record… for the shot put!"

"Aren't you just hilarious? Fine, you show me. How did you hold your arm?"

I picked up the thinnest, flattest rock I could find and reached back with my arm, waist high and parallel to the ground. Ian stepped behind me. He slid his body against mine and stretched his arm out, pressing it against my arm. The breath from his mouth, hot against my neck, stirred my hair. A shiver ran down my back when he whispered, "Like this, Jonathan?"

"Yeah, I like…um, I mean, yeah, like this. For skipping stones." My heart pounded. I stepped away and looked at Ian.

"For skipping stones, huh?" His eyes searched mine, looking for the place I never showed anyone. "Has anyone ever told you that you're really cute when you're showing off?"

The rock I'd been clutching slipped through my fingers and clattered onto the beach. Panicked, I looked around. Aaron, Sean, and Sara were sitting with a bunch of kids by the bonfire. Jake and his group were hanging down by the dock. I looked back at Ian. "Excuse me?"

"I asked if anyone has ever told you that you're cute before. Especially when you're showing off."

Sara looked in our direction. A frown passed across her face.

"Ian, what are you talking about? I'm not, you know…" My voice came out like a cross between a whisper and a hiss.

"Gay?" Though a cool breeze blew off the lake, I felt myself flush with heat.

"Yeah. I'm not gay," I whispered.

"That's good to know. Thanks for clearing that up." Ian turned his attention back to the lake. He wound his arm back again like a baseball pitcher, gripping a small boulder in his hand.

"Is that what you meant earlier? That I'd be a great junior counselor except that I'm…" I couldn't bring myself to say the word. An image of the locked safe in my bedroom flashed into my mind. For my coin collection, I'd said, when I had asked for it for

Christmas. No coins, just a couple of books. *Rainbow High*, *The Boys and The Bees*. And of course, the copy of *Boy Meets Boy*.

Reading's just a hobby. It didn't mean anything, right?

"Yeah, but it was just a crazy thought that flew through my head. I mean, of course you're not gay. You spent a whole minute sucking face with Bethany today. What gay guy does that?" Ian's voice dripped sarcasm. His arm snapped forward. The stone soared through the air and splashed into the lake. It sank deeper and deeper through the layers of water, cutting through the strong current until it probed the bottom of Spirit Lake.

I stared at the place where the rock had hit, shattering the perfect surface. The ripples expanded and drifted toward me. "Are *you* gay?" I whispered.

"What do you think?"

"I think you're terrible at skipping rocks."

"Yes, I am, Jonathan. I definitely am." He chuckled.

As the ripples eased into the vast lake, I told myself that he was only talking about his rock-skipping skills, but I knew better.

Nothing about Ian skimmed the surface.

Chapter Eight

Tuesday morning I woke up to the sound of rain hammering the roof. The cabin smelled of wet dirt as I crawled out of my sleeping bag and shivered.

Jake lumbered down the bunk-bed ladder and stood next to me, peering out the window. "Ugh, we're supposed to spend the afternoon on the lake learning how to navigate with a compass. That oughta be a blast in this shit. Hey, I heard you and that girl in Curtain Call hooked up yesterday."

"What?" When Jake made kissing sounds, I figured it out. "Oh, you mean Bethany? No, I definitely did not hook up with her. It was just part of a stupid game of Truth or Dare."

"Awesome." Jake smiled, unusual for him any time of the day, but especially before noon. "She was my partner during Silent Introductions. Does she ever talk about me?"

I looked at him in surprise. Before I had time to think, a loud laugh burst from my mouth.

A hurt look flashed over his face.

"No, Jake. That's not what I meant. I was laughing about your—"

"Iron Man pj's? Really Jake?" Fryin' Bryan—a new camper who earned the nickname by bringing an electric mosquito zapper to camp—had looked over when I laughed and apparently spotted Jake's getup too.

"Up yours, small-fry." The hard shell returned to Jake's face.

"Seriously, dude. Tell me your mom gave you those for a Christmas gift and you had to bring them." Bryan didn't relent.

"Keep it up and they'll be digging that mosquito zapper out of your ass." Jake took a step toward Bryan.

"And that's enough, all of you." The mellow melted off Aaron who pulled himself up to his full height. "One more word from either of you and you'll be scrubbing the camp toilets."

"It was just a joke," Bryan mumbled.

"I'm sorry. I really am." I tried to connect eyes with Jake, but he shoved past me. I gave up, threw my clothes on, grabbed my rain jacket, and headed out of the cabin toward the dining hall for breakfast.

❖

I pulled open the doors and inhaled the scents of applewood and cinnamon in the lodge. Elk and deer heads were mounted on the walls. Antler chandeliers hung from the ceiling and cast the room in muted light. The far end of the large room served as the indoor hangout for the camp, complete with a jukebox and bookshelves filled with every board game imaginable and dozens of puzzles—some of which even had all the pieces. Comfortable chairs and tables were scattered around, and in the corner a fire roared in the stone fireplace. The end of the room nearest the entrance boasted pine tables lined in three long rows and served as the dining hall. Soggy campers bent over their bowls of steaming oatmeal and chatted about the crappy weather. I scanned the crowd.

Plenty of redheads, just not the right one.

I shook the rain from my raincoat, then made my way through the breakfast line, grabbing a bowl of warm oatmeal. I tossed on a few raisins just for fun.

Hannah winked at me as she handed me a glass of orange juice. "Someone's been saving you a seat, I think." She nodded in the direction of a table where Bethany sat. "She's a sweet girl, Jonathan."

"Good morning," Bethany said as I sat down across from her. Her cheeks were flushed pink.

She studied her bowl like there was going to be a final exam. Her spoon carved a groove in her oatmeal. Around and around the groove, her spoon traveled. Getting nowhere fast.

"Morning. Some weather, huh?" I tried to break the tension.

"No kidding. Yuck. At least I have a cooking class with Hannah this morning, so I get to be inside. How about you?" She pulled her eyes off the bowl and looked at me.

"No such luck. Sculpture in the outdoor pavilion." Jake walked by, scowling at me like he was considering smashing his tray over my head. I shoveled in a huge bite of oatmeal. It hit my tongue and exploded like napalm, a hundred times worse than when she'd kissed me. "Ooh, ouch! Shi—shoot, that was hot."

"Oh, are you okay?" She touched my arm.

"Yeah, I'm fine. No big deal." I looked up just as Ian walked in and spotted me sitting there with Bethany's hand resting on my arm. He swiveled and walked out of the dining hall.

Presumably, he'd lost his appetite.

I know I had.

❖

I didn't bother explaining to Bethany why I grabbed my raincoat and bolted out the door. The rain had painted the camp in shades of gray. Rain dripped off every surface. I spotted him walking ahead of me.

"Hey, Ian." I sprinted to catch up with him. "Hold up. I'll walk with you."

He swung around. "Did you have a nice breakfast with your girlfriend?"

"What are you talking about? I don't have a girlfriend."

"You might want to break that news to Bethany." He began to walk away. "Hell, break it to the whole camp. They're all gossiping about you and Bethany being an item. Did you know that?"

"Ian, wait!"

"What?" Hurt lurked in his eyes. "What do you want?"

"I don't know. I just thought you could tell me other words that rhyme with day and I could teach you how to skip rocks." I sounded pathetic.

"Take my word for it, Mr. Junior Counselor, you're better off with your girlfriend."

Heat rose inside me, chasing the damp chill away. "I would never have kissed her if you hadn't suggested that stupid game! And she is not my girlfriend. I don't even want a girlfriend!"

"Right." He stared at me. "But you're not gay."

It would have been a good parting line. Unfortunately, Ian appeared to be heading in the same direction I was as we walked across the rain-drenched camp toward the arts-and-crafts pavilion. Silence stretched between us until I couldn't stand it any longer.

"I don't know what I am," I confessed as we stepped into the pavilion and out of the rain. "I just know what I'm supposed to be."

"Let me clear things up for you then. You're a confused jerk," Ian said.

"Maybe," I countered, sitting down at a table that had ample room for two people. "But I'm not a confused jerk with a girlfriend."

Ian shot me a withering glance and headed to a seat as far away from me as possible.

Simon wheeled out of the bright yellow supply hut, covered in clay and paint. "Welcome, everyone! Before we begin, I'd like to recommend you wear your worst clothes to sculpture." He looked around the class. "This is going to get messy."

Chapter Nine

Spray painted phrases like *Christ Rocks! I'm High on God! Jesus Loves You!* covered the supply hut. Someone had written *iPod, iPhone, iPad* followed by *iPray!* Dozens of painted images of crosses, peace signs, and the letters *WWJD* completed the display. I sat at one of the tables under the covered patio that was attached to the supply hut, protected from the light drizzle of rain, and tried to avoid looking at Ian.

"There are easier classes you could have taken than sculpture." Simon held a lump of clay, which he placed on a marble block, then picked up a carving knife.

"Sculpture is not like any other art form. There is no hiding the flaws." He held the knife poised in the air and studied the clay. Minutes passed. Emotions played over Simon's face. His knife descended and sliced away a third of the clay. Working quickly, he cut, stabbed, then dropped the tools altogether and attacked the clay with his hands, twisting and wrenching away all that needed to be removed. His hands slowed and his expression softened as he began to caress the clay.

Thirty minutes later Simon put his mud-soaked hands on his wheels and pushed himself away from the table, revealing an abstract replica of the willow tree that grew along the lakeshore. It was beautiful. Graceful, somehow. I swore the long branches swayed in the breeze, reminding me of all the times I had sat under the real willow tree where I always felt invisible and protected. My throat tightened as the memory played in my mind…

It was four summers ago, my third year at Spirit Lake Bible Camp. I was twelve. It was the summer my dad had bought a boat and insisted we spend every weekend fishing until he was called up for his second deployment to Iraq. It was the summer I saw the fish suffocate in the five-loaves-and-two-fish competition. It was the summer I wore my dad's glasses.

On opening day, I stood there, listening to my mother explaining to Paul, "Jonathan's father shipped out last week. It's his second tour, you know. Anyway, they're an old pair of his dad's glasses. He refuses to take them off. Pastor Jim says we shouldn't try to make him. They're just low-level readers, so it's fine that he wears them."

"I'm so sorry for both of you." Paul's hand had strayed to my head, riffling my hair. "Don't worry. We'll keep him so busy he won't have time to be sad."

They stared at me, as if the problem were the oversized glasses that slid down my face and nose like tears. They didn't see me at all. Maybe they needed glasses.

"Come on, Jonathan, you can ride in the boat with me." Everyone had gathered at the lake for the competition. Paul was trying to keep his promise to my mother, but I was having a bad day.

"I'm not going fishing. I hate fishing," I shouted.

"I don't understand, Jonathan. Your mom told me you and your father fish every weekend." Paul shook his head.

"Forget it. I'm not going." I crossed my arms and refused to look at Paul.

"It's all right, Paul. He can stay with me." Simon pushed his wheelchair over to us. "Jonathan and I will hold down the fort while the rest of you empty the lake. Sound good, Jonathan?"

"Whatever." I wanted to yell some more. It felt good, but Simon had fixed things so I didn't have an excuse anymore.

Hours later the boats came back to shore.

Paul lifted the heavy fish buckets out of the boat and dropped one, spilling the prize catch and lake water over the ground. Tail flopping. Eyes protruding and staring.

All the kids laughed. Not at me or my glasses, but at the dying fish. Someone picked it up and tossed it to me, but my hands froze. The fish smacked me in the face, leaving a streak of slime to drip down my cheek and into my mouth. My stomach heaved.

I doubled over, hands on my knees, and blinked back the tears.

"Jonathan, what's wrong?" Paul looked at me with concern. I tried to focus on him, but he swayed. The lake turned upside down and became the sky, and I collapsed, face down in the heat, inches away from the twitching, gulping fish. With 20/20 vision I witnessed as it shuddered, lay still, and died.

Simon found me hours later, hiding beneath the canopy of the willow tree.

"May I join you?" he'd asked as he parted the willow's long branches with one hand and pushed his wheelchair forward with the other.

"Sure."

"You know, Jonathan, I can spot an artistic kid a mile away, and you, my friend, are an artistic kid. Here." He held out a camera. A bit beaten up and old, but cool. "It's yours."

"Mine? Really?" I held the camera up to my face. It banged against my glasses. I took them off and awkwardly held them in one hand and the camera in the other.

"Really. I'll keep those safe for you." I put my father's glasses in Simon's outstretched hand. He slid them into his shirt pocket. "Now, let me show you how to zoom in and out."

Everything looked blurry. Exactly how I felt. Simon put his hand over mine and twisted the lens. The overwhelming world beyond the willow branches, where death could come at any moment and steal away a fish…or even a father, disappeared. A simpler, safer world came into focus.

It had been magic. Simon's magic.

"The secret to sculpture is to learn how to listen," Simon said, interrupting my memories. "Listen well and you will hear the whisper telling you what lies trapped inside the clay. You will hear the cry for freedom. Give yourself over to it, and you will learn how to free the captive within."

I looked at the willow tree sculpture.

"Open yourself to the clay, and I promise, you will come to know God more closely than ever before. To sculpt is to experience a bit of what He must have felt as He spoke all this into being." Simon waved his hand across the whole vista of Spirit Lake, the sky, and the earth.

A tear slid down my face.

I brushed it away and saw Ian staring right at me.

"Thanks for helping with the cleanup." Simon wiped the clay from his sculpting tools.

"Sure, no problem. Where does this go?" I held the remaining block of clay.

"Up there." He pointed to the highest shelf. I reached up and put the clay where it belonged and made a mental note to show up early for sculpture to help him get set up. "Thanks. So, tell me. How is your photography coming along?"

"I just started to work in black and white. Here, take a look." Simon's beater camera had finally died. I handed him my new Nikon. He clicked through the camera's memory card, stopping to zoom in on the picture I'd taken of my mother. Her eyes were closed. Wind blew through her hair. The long branches from the willow tree filled the background. "What do you think?"

"Beautiful! You have an excellent eye. You chose just the right angle to heighten your mother's emotion. Did you take it on opening day?"

"Yeah. She had been looking at the lake. She was just so peaceful. She doesn't look like that often lately."

"I can feel her thinking. Maybe praying. But I see something else. Do you?"

"No, I just know there's something not quite right. What is it?"

"Don't just look for light. See the light. It makes all the difference."

"Okay, I'll try."

"I'm glad you're taking this class, Jonathan."

"Me too." I smiled. "Thanks, Simon."

"Anytime. See you tomorrow then."

"Yeah, see you tomorrow. 'Bye." I headed toward the beach. There was someone I needed to talk to.

❖

"Need a Kleenex?" Ian asked. He didn't look up from his notebook as I parted the branches and sat beside him under the willow tree. "I'm fresh out. Maybe Bethany has one." Shadows from the branches played across his face, a moving picture on a blank canvas.

"Not this again." I sighed dramatically. "Yeah, I kissed Bethany, but it didn't mean anything and you know that. Look me in the eyes. See if I'm not telling the truth." I half expected him to get up and walk out on me. Instead, he stared at me with his deep green eyes.

Wind, whistling through the branches, carried the light scent of fish and seaweed. He studied me for a moment, then turned his head away and stared across the lake. "Okay, I'm sorry. I was being a jerk."

"Finally, we agree on something."

"I was right about one thing though. You're better off staying away from me."

My chest tightened and hurt. To be around Ian was to be on fire. Everything burned.

We sat there, not talking, leaning against the trunk of the willow tree. My fingers traced the dark green branch-shaped shadows on the grass that reached out to us, rooting us to this place together. We sat close enough to touch, though we didn't.

"So, that sculpture guy, the one in the wheelchair, he's pretty cool. He actually lets the kids paint on his building?"

"Yeah, he does. He even encourages it. Says that if all graffiti contained such messages, the world might be a better place."

"He's right," Ian said. "How does that work? Being in a wheelchair and a counselor?"

"Funny, but I don't even think about Simon being in a wheelchair," I said.

"You know what? You are going to make one helluva junior counselor."

"What about—"

"No exceptions. These doofai would be lucky to have you."

"Doofai?" I asked him.

"Plural of doofus."

I laughed and stood up. "Hey, I'm going to say hi to Dawn. Do you want to come with me?"

"Depends. Who's Dawn?" Ian looked skeptical.

"Definitely not one of your doofai."

"You sure?" He stood up and ducked under the willow's branches with me.

"Trust me. You'll like her."

"Trust you." He grinned as we walked toward the little cabin that sat nestled at the edge of the forest. "That may be the dumbest thing I do all summer."

Chapter Ten

Dawn lives here," I said as we reached the rustic cabin with solar panels on the roof.

"Hello! Anybody home?" I held the door open for Ian and we walked into the main room. The fireplace in the corner gave off the scent of stale ash. A thin layer of dust covered the furniture, and clumps of white fur clung to the chair and were gathered in its corners.

Ian's eyes wandered from the feathered dream catcher in the window, to the snowshoes propped up in the corner, to the top-of-the-line Mac computer on Dawn's desk.

"I thought there was no Internet here."

"Technically, there isn't. Dawn works for the DNR and lives here year-round. She monitors the loon population in northern Minnesota."

Ian looked at the huge map of Spirit Lake and the surrounding forest that covered a whole wall of Dawn's living room. "So, she's not a counselor?"

"Not like the other counselors who actually live in the cabins with us, but she does teach all the nature classes."

"Huh. She must like living in the boondocks." Ian inhaled. "What's that smell? I can't place it."

"Cedar, I think. Could be sweetgrass or sage."

"Why would she burn that?"

"Dawn's originally from the Mille Lacs Band of Ojibwe reservation."

Ian looked again at the dream catcher in the window and the smudging shell containing ash with the eagle feather on the coffee table. "So is Dawn a—?"

"Native American?" I finished his question. "Yeah, she is."

"I was going to ask if she's a Christian."

"Oh yeah, she's that too."

Ian walked around the room, taking in the details of Dawn's life. He let his fingers brush over her Bible that lay open on her kitchen table. His hand rested on the elk canvas of her spirit drum. He picked up the smudging shell and sniffed the ash. "Interesting. I can't wait to meet her."

"*Boozhoo.*" Dawn stood in the doorway. Next to her was a giant white dog that weighed at least a hundred pounds. He could have pulled off intimidating if it wasn't for his wagging tail and lopsided smile. Dawn threw her heavy backpack into a corner and walked toward Ian with her hand outstretched. "I am pleased to meet you too. And you are?"

"Ian McGuire. Sorry we just walked into your home." He shook her hand and quickly put the smudging shell back on the table.

"Any friend of *Needjee*'s is a friend of mine. You are welcome here."

The giant of a dog spotted me and ran forward, taking up half of Dawn's small living room. With one leap he stood and planted his two front paws on my shoulders, nearly knocking me over with his weight and his breath. "Hey, boy, who are you?" The dog dropped to the floor. I knelt and gave him the butt scratching of a lifetime.

"*Needjee,* meet *Makwa*. The current man in my life." Dawn reached down and stroked the dog. "Isn't he a beautiful puppy?"

"Did you say puppy?"

"I certainly did. *Makwa* is six months old. He's not even fully grown."

I sized up the dog and let out a low whistle. The dog leaped on Ian who probably looked like a miniature chew toy to him.

"Oh hey, hiya!" Ian laughed. They stood eye to eye, much to the dog's delight. His tongue lashed out at Ian who tried to push him down but only managed to fall on the floor. The dog climbed on top of him and resumed licking. "Um, somebody want to help me here?" Ian flailed his arms and legs. Dog saliva dripped on his face.

"*Makwa!* Sit! Down!" He didn't listen to Dawn at all. "Oh, fine then. *Makwa, namadabin!*" Dawn commanded.

The dog obediently sat on the floor next to Ian, who gasped for breath. I reached down and offered my hands. His small hands slid into mine and I yanked. Hard. Too hard. He flew into my arms. I held him until he was steady and I was not. He pulled away and looked at me, eyebrows raised.

"He understands Ojibwe?" I deliberately turned toward Dawn.

"Oh, he understands English. He certainly knows what I'm talking about when I say *walk* or *treat.* But he only behaves when I speak in Ojibwe. Don't ask me." She shrugged. "I don't get it either, but I'm quite certain my mother is laughing somewhere. She never liked it when I spoke English." I knew Dawn came from a traditional Ojibwe family. Beyond that, nothing. Dawn rarely talked about her family.

"So, what made you decide to get the world's biggest dog for a pet?" Ian asked, wiping the dog drool from his face.

"That is a story worth hearing." We sat down at Dawn's kitchen table. "Last winter, I woke up to the screech of a great horned owl. I couldn't go back to sleep, so I got up and decided to go for a walk. I had only gone a little way when I heard a sound. The forest is full of noise, even in the dead of winter, but this sound did not belong there. Like a faint whimpering that seemed to grow weaker each time I heard it." Dawn stroked the dog's soft white fur. He drooled an adoring response. "I found him, tied up in a canvas bag with two other puppies. They had already died, but *Makwa* had fought and waited until the Great Spirit brought me to him."

"Do you mean someone just threw the puppies away? To freeze to death?" Ian's face flushed.

"That's exactly what happened."

I looked at *Makwa*: all legs and fur, ears pointing in different directions, tongue as wide as my palm, and drool that never ended.

"How could someone do that?" Ian asked.

"I can't answer that."

"What does *Makwa* mean?" I asked.

"It means little bear."

"I like that. Hello, Bear." The dog's head cocked at the sound of the name.

Dawn laughed. "Apparently he does too. Feel free to call him Bear. Maybe he'll start obeying me when I speak English, though I doubt it."

Ian leaned down to stroke Bear's head. "What those people did to you sucks. You didn't deserve that." Bear leaned forward and covered Ian's entire face with one quick lick. "Okay, well, I really need a shower now." Ian stood and walked toward the door.

"Come again, both of you. Anytime. I'm planning on taking anyone who wants to go on a nature hike. I hope you and Jonathan can make it."

"When is it?" I asked as I joined Ian by the door.

"When the day is right for such a hike. I'll let you know."

"Looking forward to it." I suddenly remembered what I'd wanted to ask her. "By the way, did Edward and Bella come back?"

"Sure did. They're nesting now." Dawn looked out her window toward the lake.

"Um, Edward and Bella? Anyone care to explain?" Ian looked from Dawn to me.

"Loons," Dawn explained. "A pair that comes back to Spirit Lake every summer to raise their family."

The corner of his lips twitched. "Edward and Bella." He laughed. "Classic."

"Now, Ian, don't look at me like that. I'm team Jacob. My predecessor named them. I would have given them much better names." Dawn picked up her binoculars from the table. "In fact, I'm going to check on them now. Care to join me?"

"We'd love to, but Ian wasn't kidding when he said he needed to take a shower. Whew." I waved my hand in front of my nose. "Plus we have a Curtain Call practice after lunch. Maybe another time?" I scratched between Bear's ears. He thumped his thick tail, sending the contents of the coffee table crashing to the ground.

"*Makwa!* Stop!" Dawn shouted, but of course he didn't. "I mean, *béka!* How many times have I told you to look before you wag?" Dawn bent to pick up the shell, the eagle feather, and the broken pieces of a mug.

"Good luck with the obedience training, Dawn."

She shot me a look of sheer hopelessness.

❖

"Dawn called you *Needjee.* Why did she do that?" Ian drilled me with questions as we walked away from Dawn's cabin.

"Sometimes she gives people Ojibwe names. Not everyone though. Just some people."

"Why you? Why *Needjee*?"

"*Needjee* means my friend. She says she knew we'd be great friends the minute she met me."

Ian looked thoughtful again. "Wait, she gives people Ojibwe names and her name is Dawn?"

"Her real name is *Waubun-anung*, which means Morning Star. Everyone butchered it her first summer here, so she said we could just call her Dawn."

"You were right. She is cool. I still can't believe someone could throw puppies away to die like that though." Ian scowled.

"At least Bear's safe. I can't imagine a better place for him than with Dawn."

"Yeah? And what about the two puppies who didn't make it? What about them?" Ian asked as we turned onto Warrior's Way. "I mean, you don't throw someone away just because you don't want them around anymore. What kind of a sick bastard does a thing like that?" He leaned forward, hands on his hips, and sucked in deep breaths of air as if he'd just run a marathon.

"Like you said, some sick bastard." I rested my hand on his shoulder. "The world's full of them."

"Tell me about it." He straightened up and looked at me. He was covered in clumps of white fur. Bear's tongue and drool had styled his hair in a Mohawk gone bad. The scent of dog breath clung to him like a cheap cologne.

"Bear sure took to you." I tried to lighten the moment as we continued to walk down the dirt path.

"Evidently." Ian wiped the remains of Bear's drool off his face.

"He was just giving you kisses. It means he likes you."

We reached the front of the shower room and stopped. "It usually does." Ian looked at me longer than necessary. He leaned forward and plucked a clump of white fur off my shirt. "Maybe you should take a shower too."

Images of the two of us alone, hot water pouring down our naked bodies, flashed through my mind. "I think I'll hit the beach instead. Go for a swim."

"You sure?" he asked.

"I'm sure." I avoided his eyes by examining the top of the tallest fir tree.

The door to the shower room squeaked open and banged shut. A shower sputtered to life, and the faint scent of soap filled the air.

Then I heard it: the sigh that escaped through the screen window, hooking me and pulling me to him.

What am I going to do with you, Ian?

I paused, listening to the sounds of water splashing, birds chirping, voices dueling inside my mind.

I walked away quickly.

Chapter Eleven

Time is different at camp. There is no Monday-through-Friday grind. Just a stream of Saturdays to float on, one after the other, like the waves on Spirit Lake. I had spent seven gold coins. The hot first week of July melted in a blur of Curtain Call meetings and sculpture classes and Bible studies and my attempts to master black-and-white photography. I took countless pictures of the sun, trying to understand what it meant to *see* light.

But my main preoccupation had become studying Ian.

I learned to recognize the tones of his voice. His default tone: dry and sarcastic. His John the Baptist tone: dramatic, some would say melodramatic. My favorite: his tender tone, rare and revealing. I studied his walk: the way he leaned into the future like he was running from the past. The way he hitched up his oversized, secondhand shorts with his left hand only to pull them down on the right side when he jammed his fist deep into his pocket. The white gash of skin that cut in around his jutting hipbone. Exposed. Vulnerable. Tempting.

Mostly I memorized his face. Sharp angles softened by a dusting of freckles. Hair that bled in the shade and combusted in the sun. Curls, like flames, that danced in the wind. Lips, top thin and bottom heavy. Made more for pouting than smiling. But oh, when he smiled!

One evening, when the sun hung low and the long stems of the pussy willows swayed in a slow dance, I walked the length of the beach, camera in hand, past Simon's pavilion and the outdoor theater. Beyond the boathouse where Paul's land ended, chasing the dying light as it glinted off the smooth surface of the lake. Hoping to capture a bit of the dusk magic.

Clambering over the barrier of rock, I reached a remote stretch of beach and sank down on the cool bed of sand. A breeze crept over my skin. The tide sloshed against the rocks. Above me, gold burst into orange and flamed in protest before it melted into indigo. I raised my camera and focused, not on the setting sun, but on the quarter moon, the rising star of night.

Then Ian spoke from someplace behind me, shattering the moment. "'Nothing Gold Can Stay.'"

Startled, I sucked in my breath and closed my eyes as the realization that he'd followed me hit me. His feet crunched through the sand until he stood next to me.

"Who's the show-off now?" I whispered. "It sorta sounds familiar."

"It's a poem by Robert Frost." He chuckled. His husky voice ignited the familiar burn again, searing me. "Guess you weren't paying attention in English class."

"Guess not."

"Want some company?"

"No, not really." I tried to lie, to sound smooth. I failed.

"Whatever." He sat next to me. I kept my eyes closed and listened to him breathe.

His hot breath tickled my face. Alarm bells sounded in my head. I clawed into the cool sand for something solid to hold on to, but it slipped through my fingers.

I jumped at his touch as I felt him tracing my eyebrow. My moan, a traitor, told all my secrets.

"I've been watching you," he said. "You're quite the joiner. So *campy*."

"I am not—"

He pressed his finger against my lips. My eyes flew open. The protest died in my mouth as I stared into his face that hovered inches above me. My stomach tightened. The indigo night swallowed the last streaks of sunlight.

"You can hide who you are from the people back there. You can even pretend to be the golden boy all you want, Jonathan. But you don't have to do that with me."

"I don't?" It wasn't really a question. I saw the truth reflected in his eyes. He saw me. The real me.

"No, you don't." He leaned closer. Just a breath between us. "Truth or Dare?"

"Truth, definitely truth." After the fiasco on the pontoon, I'd never choose dare. Ever. Again.

"Do you want me to kiss you?"

I groaned. This game sucked. "Yes."

His lips brushed mine. Light. No pressure. Except for the volcano that swelled inside of me.

"I'm going to go now," Ian whispered.

"Yeah, I think that's a good idea." I listened to the sound of his retreating footsteps, crunching in the sand.

❖

Later, alone in the boys' shower room, I brushed the sand from my feet and legs and stared at the stranger in the metal mirror. Dark brown hair. Scandalously long and disobedient. Dull brown eyes. Lips that sinned by telling the truth.

Light glinted off the gold cross that hung from my neck. One hard yank and the chain broke. The cross landed on the grimy floor.

The boy in the mirror was still a stranger. But at least he wasn't a liar.

CHAPTER TWELVE

The sand volleyball score was tied, three to three. Jake, Aaron, and I were playing Ian, Sean, and Bryan. It was my turn to serve when Paul emerged from the administration building and waved at me. I dropped the ball and walked off the court.

"C'mon, Coop! We got this. Where are you going now?" Jake called after me. I waved to let him know I'd be right back as I jogged over to Paul.

"Jonathan, your mom's on the phone." My stomach tightened as I followed him into the office. "Everything's fine. She wanted me to tell you that right away."

"Thanks, Paul." I sat on the chair and picked up the phone. "Hey, Mom. What's up?"

"Hi, Jon! Your dad just called. His platoon is someplace in the al-Anbar province in Iraq. He couldn't give me more details."

"How did he sound?"

"Fine. He told me to tell you that you're the man of the house until he gets home." Her words ran together the way they do when she's nervous. "He asked me to pray for him, can you believe that?"

I couldn't, actually. My father always said he'd seen too much blood to believe in God.

Mom and I were the believers. Prayer warriors: fighting the same battle, just in our own way.

"It's silly, I suppose, but I wanted to tell you he's safe and see if we could pray together."

"That's not silly, Mom. Let's pray now." My hand reached for my neck, naked without my cross. I felt his lips against mine. My head sank into my hands and I curved my whole body around the phone, hugging her across the distance.

"Heavenly Father, thank You for allowing us news about Jonathan's father," Mom began. "You know where he is and what danger surrounds him. Please, Lord, send Your angels to protect him. Keep him safe and bring him home to us. Amen." Mom's voice grew stronger and calmer as she prayed. Her faith wrapped around her like a warm blanket on a freezing night.

"Amen." I shivered.

"I love you, Jon."

"I love you too. It's going to be okay. This is Dad, right? He'll have the bad guys running in no time." I forced myself to laugh.

She chuckled. "He sure will. I'm going to let you go now so you can get back to having fun. Please thank Paul for me."

"I will. Call if you hear anything else. Love you, Mom." I placed the phone receiver on its cradle and then I remembered. Al-Anbar. My father had called it the hornet's nest, the heart of the jihad movement, the birthplace and cradle of al-Qaeda. The phone call could have brought much different news.

Tears snuck down my cheeks. Paul squeezed my shoulders and stood beside me, whispering a prayer. I took a deep breath and stood up.

"Thanks."

"No problem. This is your dad's third tour, right?"

"Yeah."

"I know you're proud of him, Jonathan. I also know how hard this is on you and your mom. I'm keeping your whole family in my prayers." Paul pulled me in for one of his famous bear hugs.

I walked back to the volleyball court, but my heart wasn't in it. I pictured Mom, curled into Dad's giant La-Z-Boy chair, crying into a cup of cold coffee.

"Everything okay?" Aaron tossed the ball to me.

"Yeah, everything's fine," I lied. Across the net, I felt Ian's eyes on me. His face was a question mark.

"All right, Coop! Enough farting around then. Let's slaughter these wimps!" Jake shouted. Nodding, I tossed the ball up into the air.

Chapter Thirteen

The phone call played itself over and over in my mind the next morning at Curtain Call. I sat next to Ian, stealing sideways glances at him, remembering our kiss.

Lily reported on how the costumes were coming. "Hannah and I are almost finished. The robes are done, and King Herod's beard that Hannah made is amazing. I can't wait to see it on Jonathan."

"Me either." Bethany reached up to stroke my cheek.

Jake walked up, holding a script. Beside me, Ian groaned. "What's he doing here?"

"Guess what?" Sara interrupted Lily's costume report. "I stole Jake from Outdoor Rec."

"I bet she bribed him with doughnuts," Ian whispered. His breath brushed against my face.

"Yeah, you're probably right." My voice sounded flat, even to me.

"What's wrong?" Ian looked right through me.

"Nothing," I said, but I could tell by his face that he didn't buy it.

Sara threw a glance in our directions. *Shut it,* she said with her eyes. "It was clear at our meeting the other day that our guys are outnumbered. I asked Jake if he would be willing to help us out and—praise the Lord!—he agreed."

Jake grinned and sat down in the circle next to Bethany.

Sara continued, "I need to get together with the girls for a second and talk dance moves. Guys, why don't you fill Jake in on the play?" Sara walked behind the costume hut with the girls, leaving Jake with us.

In the distance I heard MacKenzie's raised voice. "Seriously, Bethany, is that your idea of a seductive dance? You've got to grind your hips, girl! Here, let me show you how."

"Did she say dance?" Jake frowned. "Nobody said anything about dancing. I ain't dancing."

"You don't have to," I promised. "Just Bethany dances."

Jake looked relieved, then intrigued. "How much for a lap dance?" He leered.

"You're an asshole," Ian stated.

"What's your issue? You got a hard-on for Bethany?"

"Hardly. She's not my type."

"That's what I figured. I doubt any of the girls here are your type," Jake sneered.

Ian dropped his gaze.

"So, what did she promise you?" I attempted to lighten the moment. "Was it doughnuts?"

"Doughnuts? Are there doughnuts?" Jake looked around.

"Not today. So what did she promise you?"

"She said I'd get to chop someone's head off." A malicious smile spread over Jake's face.

"Fabulous," Ian muttered, opening his script. "Just fabulous."

❖

"Okay, crew, our first priority now is to get off script." Sara returned with the girls. Bethany looked miserable. "Also, we have a few logistical issues we need to figure out. When I wrote this, I envisioned a large dining hall filled with King Herod's guests. Jake helps fill out our numbers, but we're still undercast big-time."

"No, we're not." Ian surprised everyone. "Not if we include the audience."

"I think I see where you're going with this, but could you elaborate?" Sara asked.

"We could set up tables and chairs for the audience, sort of like a dinner theater, and we could have baskets of Hannah's bread and glasses of grape juice to look like wine. That way the audience becomes part of the play by being Herod's dinner guests."

"That's brilliant!" Sara grinned. "Ian, speak up if you get any more ideas like that. Lily, would you talk to Hannah about what we'll need for the dinner props?"

I looked at Ian with surprise. Was this the guy who had called me a joiner?

"Sure, Sara. I could even help Hannah bake the bread."

"So, that's one challenge easily overcome. Now for the other—and this one is a bit, well, bloodier. How are we going to handle presenting Ian's head on a platter?"

"I vote for decapitation," Jake said. "One chop with an ax and there you go, perfect prop."

"Gross!" MacKenzie shot Jake a dirty look. "Tell me again why you're here?"

"Because someone needs to chop his head off." Jake motioned toward Ian.

"Jake is right about one thing." Sara interrupted the bickering. "We do need to make the audience believe that John the Baptist has been beheaded. Any thoughts on how we can accomplish that?"

"We could put a cantaloupe on a platter and cover it with a cloth. Wouldn't the audience believe it's Ian's head?" Kari suggested.

"I guess I envisioned something a bit more gruesome," Sara said.

Bethany spoke up. "Maybe Simon could sculpt a bust of Ian's head. I know he could paint it to look realistic. Just imagine the audience when Jake walks out with that on a platter!"

"That's a great idea."

"I have another idea, Sara," Ian suggested. "It's a blending of both Bethany's and Kari's ideas. What if we had Jake bring out a platter with the bust hidden underneath the cloth? The audience would naturally imagine my head, but they'd also probably be thinking it's a cantaloupe or something equally non-scary under the cloth. Then someone pulls the cloth off, and they see Simon's sculpture when they're not expecting it."

This time I did mouth the words *so campy* at him. He grinned and flipped me off by rubbing his nose with his middle finger.

Curtain Call ended with the problems of dinner guests and beheadings fixed, thanks to Ian who walked up to me afterward, still in problem-solving mode.

"Hey, what's up? And don't lie and say nothing, because that's a bunch of bullshit."

"Okay, you're right."

"Let's go talk about it then."

"Not here." Everywhere I looked: people, people, and more people.

"I have an idea." Ian grinned. "Follow me."

It took Ian less than three minutes to talk Sean into letting us take a canoe out. Impressive. The sound of the lake, lapping against the sides of the canoe as it sliced through Spirit Lake, filled the silence that settled over us. We set course for the far opposite shore. The breeze was light. The tension drained from my body, as if it traveled down my arms, through my hands, along my oar, and into the lake. We stopped paddling and let the canoe coast into a garden of lily pads that grew along the opposite shore. I rested the oar over my legs and reached out with my hands. The tips of the lilies brushed against my palms. Tiny frogs, perched on the pads, took one look at us and dove into the water.

Ian swiveled his legs over the bench and looked at me. "So, talk to me."

"I don't know where to begin." How could I tell him about my father, risking his life in Iraq, while I calmly sat in a canoe, laughing at frogs?

"Something changed when Paul called you into the office yesterday." Was there anything he didn't notice? Talk about annoying.

"My mom called. She heard from my dad. He made it safely to Iraq."

Ian's eyes widened. "Safely to Iraq? Is there such a thing?"

"I don't think so. But he's a Marine. He knows how to take care of himself."

"Marine, huh? That explains a lot."

"What do you mean?"

"I knew you were from a military family, Mr. Junior Counselor. Always ready to defend the underdog. Of course you're the kid of a Marine. You practically have *Semper Fi* tattooed on your forehead. Just like your dad—a born hero." He grinned.

"I'm nothing like my dad." My voice cracked. "But while he's gone, I'm in charge. The man of the house. And where am I? Mowing the lawn for my mom? Helping her with the grocery shopping? The fence needs painting, but I'm not painting it because I'm floating around in this dumb canoe."

"So go home."

"I don't want to!" The words burst from me. "I don't want to be home. I don't want to be the man of the house. I just want to be—"

"What?"

"Here."

"So stay. Stay with me."

Nearby, a loon yodeled. Too close. "Ian, we need to leave. I think Edward and Bella are nesting near here."

"That'd be cool to see." Ian peered past the lily pads toward the long marsh grasses that grew along the shore.

"You don't understand." I plunged my paddle into the lake. The canoe moved away from the shore. "We could scare them. They could abandon their nest and their babies."

Bella floated into view. On her back were two brown fuzzy babies. Edward pulled himself upright and tucked his wings against his body, propelling himself furiously toward us with his feet.

"What's he doing?" Ian laughed.

"It's called the penguin dance. He thinks we're a threat to his family so he's trying to scare us away. He won't stop until we leave or he dies of exhaustion." I didn't find anything funny about the situation.

Ian read my face, swiveled in his seat, and thrust his oar into the water. Our canoe shot forward. Edward relaxed and sank onto the lake.

"Not to be negative or anything, but you do know things got pretty weird for Edward and Bella, right?"

"Yeah, I know." I stared across the lake.

CHAPTER FOURTEEN

"Oh man, is it early." I yawned. Two days had passed since we had taken the canoe out. Four days since the kiss. Four long days locked in an orbit around Ian and four long nights of constant dreams. Some were about the war—my father, walking into a building minutes before it blew up. Others were about Ian. Those were rated R or higher. I prayed every night. For the dreams to stop. For Jesus to protect my dad. For strength to fight my feelings. The carved letters *WWJD* on the bunk above me demanded an answer I didn't have. I even searched the bathroom for my cross, but it was gone. Swept up with all my good intentions and tossed away.

Day after day we grew closer. To each other. To impact.

I knew I should run.

Instead, Ian came up with an idea to take my mind off my dad and asked me to meet him in the dining hall.

"This is your idea of fun? Hauling me out of bed before six a.m.? Sorry, but I'm not sure this is keeping my mind off anything since I'm still half-asleep."

"Quit your griping." Ian grinned. "Besides, you'll cheer up when you hear my news. I found us a private place where we can meet. It's about twenty feet away from the highest ridge of the trail that goes around Spirit Lake. The offshoot to it is so hidden no one else would be able to find it."

I lifted my head off the table. Private place? My heart began to thud again. Terror and temptation: the twins that had invaded my mind. "An offshoot to a hidden place? How come I don't know about it?"

"I only found it because I was following a porcupine," Ian said, impressed with himself. Wanting me to be impressed as well.

I blinked as his words registered. "I know it's early, but did you say you were following a porcupine?"

"Yup."

"Tell me there's more to this story." Curiosity began to gnaw at me.

"I had to get away from camp for a bit. Don't you ever feel like that?"

"Sure, sometimes."

"So, I was exploring the forest and saw a porcupine cruising down a path. I followed him, but he disappeared into a bush. When I knelt, I discovered a small opening. Of course I had to check it out."

"Of course you did."

"When I came out on the other side, I found myself in this clearing that has the most perfect view of the camp. It's unbelievable. I mean, we can see everything that's happening here, but they can't see us at all. It's like looking down on the inside of an anthill. It's totally private. We're going. Right after breakfast."

"Hey!" Bethany walked into the dining hall and sat next to me. "What are you guys doing up so early?"

"Ask him," I grumbled.

"Jonathan's not a morning person." Ian blew off her question. If I'd been more awake, I would have busted him on it. "What are you doing here so early?"

"Hannah's baking cinnamon rolls for breakfast. It's a big job so I volunteered to help her."

"That's nice of you," I said.

"She's going to give me her recipe." Bethany grinned. "I'd better get into the kitchen now. Jonathan, do you want to go for a canoe ride after breakfast?" She placed her hand on my arm. She smiled. Ian didn't.

"Sorry, but Jonathan and I made a date to memorize our lines after breakfast." Ian used his innocent tone. He reached beneath the table and squeezed my leg.

"I need to do that too. Can I join you?" Bethany's fingers stroked my arm.

"We're concentrating on the Herod/John the Baptist scene. Maybe another time." Ian smiled, squeezing tighter.

"Oh, okay then. Another time. 'Bye guys." Bethany walked into the kitchen. The smell of baking bread filled the dining room.

"*We made a date?*" I hissed at Ian. "What are you *thinking*?"

"That it would be nice to get away with you today. Alone."

I breathed a sigh of relief as the dining hall filled up for breakfast. After Paul's prayer, Ian got in line for breakfast, but I stayed and passed. I already had plenty to digest.

We waited for thirty minutes after breakfast, pretending to practice our lines in the dining hall. Truthfully, we were waiting for Hannah to finish cleaning the dishes and leave her kitchen ripe for the raiding, as Ian said.

"You're not going swimming?" Hannah asked as she walked through the dining hall.

"No." Ian lied with ease. "I burn too easily."

Hannah took one look at his pale complexion and accepted the answer without question.

"You guys can stay as long as you like. Just close up when you leave, okay?"

"Sure, Hannah. No problem." The twinges of guilt struck me. We waited another ten minutes, just to be safe, before we snuck into the kitchen.

"I'm still not sure about this," I said as a strawberry-rhubarb pie and a six-pack of root beer disappeared into Ian's backpack. "Hannah would give us the food if we just asked her."

"Yeah, she probably would, but then you'd be missing the whole point."

"And the point is?"

The sound of whistling sent us scrambling out of the kitchen. Ian grabbed a bag of Doritos and flew out the door with me two steps behind him. *This is crazy*, I thought, *Crazy, but fun!* Which, of course, was Ian's point.

Ian alternated sauntering with sudden bursts of sprinting toward the edge of the woods. He could have passed for Mike Myers in a corny Austin Powers movie minus the tuxedos, the hot girls, and the cool British accent.

"You're insane!" I laughed as we ducked into the forest. Ian doubled over, panting. "I mean, you're certifiable! You should have seen yourself!"

"Me? What about you? I've seen less guilty-looking criminals on *America's Most Wanted*. C'mon, this way to Porcupine Point."

The light in the woods loved Ian. It fell on him and turned his red hair into an open flame that could spark a forest fire at any moment. I followed him up a steep incline. The rocks were slippery, covered in lime-green moss, and beautiful against the rich black dirt of the trail. Ian led us down a path I didn't know. I scanned for landmarks, anything that might tell me where we were. When I looked back, Ian had disappeared.

"Ian? Where are you?"

"You've got to come through here." He stuck his hand out and waved through a nearly invisible gap in the bushes.

"You're kidding, right?"

"Nope. It's bigger than it looks."

I knelt and crawled through the opening. My head bashed into something hard.

"Shit! I didn't tell you to barge through. Crap!"

I couldn't help but laugh as I crawled through the bush and found Ian sprawled on his butt, scowling and rubbing his forehead.

"Wow!" Stepping into the clearing felt just like finding hidden treasure I didn't have to share. Except with Ian, and he was part of the treasure.

"I know, right?"

I crossed the patch of grass in a dozen steps, stood at the edge of the cliff, and looked across Spirit Lake. I felt Ian move behind me. He made no noise and I didn't look at him, but I felt him coming closer to me. That's the way it had become with us. Orbiting. Always orbiting. Vertigo hit as I looked at the rocks below and imagined falling hard. The waves pounded, splashing against the shore, wearing down even the strongest of rocks. I sat down on the grassy edge where I couldn't fall or jump.

We were right across from camp. Far enough away that we were invisible to anyone who happened to look in our direction. I leaned back to take in the full view of the sprawling sky above me.

"So who exactly is this John the Baptist guy?" Ian sat down next to me.

"Wow. I guess I just assumed you knew who John the—"

Ian raised an eyebrow and frowned at me.

"I know, I know. Erroneous assumptions, right? Let's see, who's John the Baptist? He's from the New Testament. He traveled around telling people the Messiah had come. A lot of people didn't want to hear that, so John had a tough life. He lived in the wilderness a lot and looked kind of wild."

"What was his beef with Herod?"

"Basically John the Baptist got in trouble for saying that it was against God's commandments for Herod to get divorced and marry his brother's ex-wife."

"Sounds like this John the Baptist had a big mouth."

"What can I say? Sara has a gift for perfect casting." He walked right into it.

"Ouch." Ian laughed, easy and light. He threaded his fingers through mine like it was the most natural thing in the world. "So, they were both divorced when they got married?"

"Yup. That's the story."

"I don't get it. Divorced people remarry all the time. No one has a hissy fit about it."

"Yeah, but that's now. The Bible was written thousands of years ago. Things were different back then."

Ian thought for a few moments. "So the Bible is outdated."

I pulled my hand away and stared at him.

"It must be if we can get divorced now, but we couldn't then. What else could it be? Unless God changed His mind."

"God doesn't change His mind. God is constant." A wave crashed against the rocks below.

"Something changed, Jonathan."

Ian's logic hit me hard. "I'm not sure. I've never thought about it before. We could ask Paul. He'd know the answer."

"Pass." Ian rolled his eyes. "You hungry yet?"

"Starving."

"Too bad we only brought one pie and it's all mine." Ian sprang up and ran toward the backpack.

"No way!" I was right behind him.

He reached the pie first. Of course he did.

"Open up." Ian leaned forward, scooping a huge forkful of strawberry-rhubarb decadence and waving it in front of my face.

I leaned forward, parted my lips, and an explosion of tart and sweet hit my tongue. Saliva flooded my mouth, and I tried not to think about how Ian feeding me pie didn't feel the slightest bit like being a kid. It felt like being a man. With a man.

"Want more?" he asked in that damned sexy way he had of layering meanings.

I nodded.

"Close your eyes," he instructed.

"Why?"

"Because everything is better with your eyes closed."

The statement was ridiculous, but not as ridiculous as the fact that I obeyed and waited for what I knew was going to happen. At least his lips tasted like strawberry rhubarb.

And so we took turns, feeding each other bites of pie and kisses until there was no more pie and no more excuse for our game.

"Get away!" I waved my hand at the bees that crawled over the empty pie plate. The sound of their buzzing filled my ears.

"Let them be and come over here." Ian leaned against the tree trunk, not even trying to hide the bulge in his shorts.

I looked away from him. The bees swarmed the pie plate, a mass of yellow-and-black bodies crawling over each other, sucking at the sweet smears of syrup.

"You think it's safe?" I ran my fingers through my hair and wished for better words. "Ignoring the fact that at any moment we could both get stung?"

"I can handle it," he said, and I believed him. He could handle it.

I also knew I wasn't him. "I don't know if I can."

Ian stood and picked up the pie plate. He walked to the edge of the cliff and hurled it. For a moment it hung in the air, suspended, like a UFO before crashing on the rocks below. The bees never moved. They could have flown away at any moment, but instead they rode the plate to their doom, intent on only one thing: satisfying their need. He turned to look at me, expectation written in his eyes.

I opened my script. "We should practice our lines for Curtain Call."

Ian sighed and lay down in the shade of a tree. "Nope, no can do. I need to digest." He peeled off his T-shirt, bunched it up under his head, and closed his eyes.

My eyes crawled over his face, along the ridge of his collarbone, across his thin, defined chest and his ribs that jutted out. Over his pink nipples and down to his belly button and beyond.

"Okay, but we shouldn't wait too long. Sara's going to expect us to have these lines down soon."

"I agree. We shouldn't wait too long." Ian yawned and stretched his arms out. "Parents' day will be here before you know it. Now will you come over here if I promise not to bite?"

Ian's arm was too skinny to really be a comfortable pillow, but that didn't stop me from resting my head on it. It didn't stop me from discovering that he was right. Again. Everything was better with your eyes closed. Kisses, pie, dreams of kisses and pie, and before I knew what had happened, I woke up hours later, Ian's legs and arms flung over me, to the grating buzzing sound of ravenous mosquitoes.

"Ian, we fell asleep!" Without thinking, I put my hands on his chest and tried to shake him awake. A current ran over his smooth skin. One touch shocked me even more awake.

"Shit! What time is it?" He sat up, eyes wide open.

"I don't know." I looked at the sinking sun. "Maybe seven? They'll be wondering about us."

Ian pulled his shirt over his head and shoved the empty root beer cans in his backpack. We sprinted through the forest. Along the upper trail, down the mossy rocks to the lower trail. Our feet pounded against the dirt path. Out of breath and swatting at angry red welts, we tried to act cool as we walked into the dining hall. The scent of Tater Tot hot dish hung in the air. A light chatter buzzed in the background. The dining hall was nearly empty. The main swarm had already left. Hannah was just beginning to clear her serving line.

"Would you boys like a slice of strawberry-rhubarb pie?" Hannah asked, a knowing glint in her narrowed sky-blue eyes. Her fists planted on her wide hips. Only her smile betrayed her good nature. "Or have you already had one?"

"Thanks, Hannah, we're good." I shot an accusing glance at Ian.

"Are you now?" Hannah plopped a scoop of steaming hot dish on our plates. "I'm not so sure about that."

"Oh, we're good, but we're not half as good as your strawberry-rhubarb pie, Hannah," Ian said, taking a piece of pie.

"You nearly got us into trouble," I hissed as we sat down and looked at my sparse tray, regretting that I'd passed on Hannah's pie.

"There's no such thing as nearly." Ian took a bite of pie. "For example, you *nearly* had another slice of pie. I doubt that's much comfort though."

"Loser."

"Do I have to remind you again to stop talking about yourself? It's quite narcissistic."

"Whatever."

"Regretting our getaway?"

"Um, let's see. We almost got in trouble, I'm covered in mosquito bites, you murdered a bunch of bees, and everyone is probably wondering where we were all afternoon. What do you think?"

"Are you?"

"No, not at all." I held his eyes.

"Good. Me neither." Ian pushed his half-eaten slice of pie over to me. "Besides, you've got to admit it worked. You didn't think about him once today."

"Who?"

"Your dad."

"No, I didn't. Not once." I swallowed hard.

"Lighten up. You're allowed to have some fun, you know."

Ian smiled at me. A hot flush spread across my cheeks.

"Speaking of which, meet me tonight once everyone in your cabin is asleep. Down by the lake where I found you before. Oh, and bring a towel."

"Okay, but why?"

"Because we're going skinny-dipping."

My jaw dropped in astonishment, but no words came out. My mind went blank. I picked up a fork and took a bite of Ian's pie, the aftertaste of strawberry and sin lingering in my mouth.

Chapter Fifteen

I lay in my bunk, listening to the sounds of heavy, rhythmic breathing and Jake's thundering snore.

Should I?

The crickets were tuning up their wings. Their songs floated on the night breeze that slipped through the screen window, stirring my imagination. In the moist sand, burrowed deep in their amphitheater holes, they called for their mates. They were not alone.

I pulled the zipper on my sleeping bag open, freed my legs, and felt for my towel in the darkness. Aaron looked sound asleep. What explanation could I possibly give if he woke up and noticed I had snuck out?

I inched the door open to avoid creaking and slipped out of the cabin, clutching my towel and my vow to be truthful. Consequences be damned.

I found him sitting just as I had imagined him, on the shore. Leaning far back, face to the night sky, deep in thought. It wasn't too late to go back to the safety of my cabin, I knew, but the cricket song drew me. It filled me until I was part of it. Lost in it.

"Hey." I stood on a rock and looked down on him.

"You came." He turned at my voice. "I wasn't sure you were going to."

"Me either." I jumped off the rock and walked over to him. Ian's pale skin glowed to near transparency, making him look even more fragile than usual. He shivered though the night felt muggy. An urge to put my arms around him hit me.

"It's official." Ian stood up and pulled his shirt over his head. One quick yank and his oversized shorts fell around his ankles. He stepped out of them. He was going commando. "You're not junior-counselor material anymore."

I looked. You bet I looked. He was a thin torch, glowing in the moonlight. My stomach tightened. The palms of my hands throbbed and grew moist with sweat.

Ian stepped into the lake. "The water's perfect." He faced me, backing into the lake.

Turn away! Run! the voice in my head screamed, but I froze, eyes fixed on Ian. *His whole body is covered in freckles,* I thought. *A reflection of the stars above.* The water covered his ankles. Two steps back. His knees. Two more. His thighs. Three more steps. The shudder started in his belly and rippled up his chest. He gasped. I knew why. Every guy knows why. At least I could breathe again. He flung himself backward into the lake. His naked body cut the surface. He went under, immersing himself.

Now, move! I ripped off my shorts, my shirt, kicked off my sandals and plowed into the lake. My legs churned the water. It flew in every direction. I pushed against the resistance, leading with my heart until I reached him.

"Jeez! Be quiet, will ya? You sounded like a herd of buffalo splashing into the lake."

Water lapped over my shoulders. We were two bobbing heads, one aflame. The other, dark as coal. I looked toward the remote beach for any sign of movement. "Do you think someone heard me?" Our clothes, indisputable evidence, lay crumpled on the shore.

"If they did, they'd probably just think a fish jumped. Or a thousand." Ian rode the waves. Up and down.

"Let's hope so." *We need to be quiet,* I tried to convince myself, *that's the only reason we're huddled so close together.* My hands and legs fluttered. Keeping me afloat. Ian's arm brushed against me as he swam in place. Shivers shot through me like a burst of adrenaline. The water swirled around me like a million naughty fingers. Beneath the water, I felt myself respond.

"So, now what?" I whispered. He drew closer. Our noses bumped awkwardly.

"What do you mean, now what?"

"I've never been skinny-dipping before. What do you do?" A wave swelled and caught me with my mouth open. "Yuck." I spit out the lake water that tasted like worms and fish poop.

Ian grinned in the darkness. "You stop thinking for once and let yourself be a part of nature. It's even better in the daytime. You don't even need the lake. You just lie out on the grass and feel the sun on your naked body."

"You've done this during the day? Walked around naked? Outside?" I pictured what would happen if I tried that in my suburban backyard.

"Sure. All the time. Dairy cows have tails…they don't tell them."

"Poor cows!" One strong thrust and I dunked him. He came up sputtering and retaliating. His thin arms and legs wrapped around me. I felt him, hot and hard, against my thigh. I struggled, but he was strong. The night sky and all its blinking witnesses disappeared as he pulled me under into a silent world. His arms changed from crushing to gentle; his head rested on my chest. He traced the small dip in my lower back with his fingers, sending shivers racing up my spine.

My head broke the surface, and I gasped for air. Ian emerged. He tossed his head, spraying me with lake water. Curls hung into his eyes that asked a question I had no clue how to answer.

"It's late." Beneath the water I traced his hip and thigh, soft just like I knew it would be. He pulled me close. I closed my eyes and felt his mouth on my neck, above my pounding pulse. Hot. Burning.

"Stay with me, Jonathan." He pleaded with his eyes.

I broke away. My arms sliced the water, carving out distance between us. My feet kicked, desperate to reach the shore. I stumbled up the beach and pulled on my clothes.

I ran.

I tiptoed into the cabin, dark and silent as a tomb, and hung my towel on the railing of my bunk bed. I zipped myself into my body-hugging sleeping bag where I tossed and turned. Plagued by memories.

Trapped inside a cocoon, I felt myself changing.

But into what?

I closed my eyes and prayed for sleep, even dared to ask for the answer to the question. In the deepest hours of night, my pillow dampened from my wet hair and tears, the answer finally came to me.

I was becoming the stranger in my mirror.

❖

Sleep did not come easily that night. Or the next. Or the next.

Trying to avoid Ian was impossible. I saw him everywhere. At Curtain Call. In the dining hall. Under the willow tree. Sculpting with Simon. In my dreams when I closed my eyes at night. Everywhere.

I tossed in my bunk, thinking of the gold coins that remained in my pocket. Only fifteen, and I couldn't decide how I should spend them: running away from Ian or running toward him.

"Yo, Cooper, will you quiet down?" Jake's voice boomed through the dark cabin, shattering the crickets' symphony on the third night since the skinny-dipping incident. "What's up with you tonight? Did you squat in some poison ivy or something?"

I finally broke free, struggled to my feet, and grabbed my jacket and flashlight.

"Everything okay, Jonathan?" Aaron's voice in the darkness stopped me.

"Yeah, I just need to get away by myself for a bit. You know, think about a few things and pray."

"Okay. Want company?" Aaron propped himself up on an elbow. Moonlight shone on his face.

"Not tonight. Thanks." I walked out of the cabin and wandered through the dark forest. Hooting sounds echoed around and above me. I crawled through the opening to Porcupine Point and stepped into the refuge that had become, somehow, ours. Moonlight painted the clearing in broad strokes of blue and black. The flickering light from hundreds of fireflies guided me to the edge of the cliff.

There was no sky and lake anymore. Just one perfectly reflecting the other.

An image of Ian sprang into my mind. A breeze swept off the lake and penetrated my thin jacket. Shivers ran over my flesh.

"Lord"—I closed my eyes and prayed—"please hear my prayer." I sat on the edge of the cliff, plagued by doubts. "All my life I've heard stories about You and how You love me. You've always been there for Mom and me. You've kept Dad safe. But I don't know what these feelings mean. Lord, I am so confused." Waves splashed against the rocks below me. The warbling hooting grew louder, closer.

"Come to me, Lord Jesus." I sent the invitation out into the stars. The cool fingers of the night air caressed my face. Beneath me Spirit Lake hummed its constant song. The mismatched puzzle pieces of my life swam in my mind: Mom and Dad, Pastor Jim, the guys on my soccer team at East Bay Christian Academy, even dreams I'd had for my future. A girl in white walked toward me, holding a bouquet of flowers tied with a satin ribbon. She looked like Bethany. Other images came to my mind: Ian with his freckled nose buried in his notebook, the feel of his fingers as they traced the small of my back, his mouth on my neck, my lips. My head sank into my hands. Tears dripped between my fingers and plunged toward Spirit Lake. There were two puzzles. It was impossible to make them fit together.

All things are possible to him who believes in Me. The voice came to me on the night breeze.

"I do believe in You!" I lifted my head to Heaven.

The air around me stilled.

Nothing can separate you from My love, child.

The sound of rustling leaves from the bush with the hidden entrance broke the spell. *Ian?* I feared…I hoped.

"*Boozhoo, Needjee.*" Dawn and Bear stepped into our clearing. Dawn's features disappeared in the darkness of the night, but Bear glowed like an angel.

"Hey, Dawn. What are you guys doing out here?" I wiped the tears from my eyes.

"This is one of my favorite spots. Especially when I need a quiet place to think."

"It is? I never even knew about it. Ian found it."

"Ian?"

"Yeah, my friend. The short guy with the red hair. The one that Bear likes so much."

"Ah, I call him *Migasowinini*."

"What does that mean?"

"It means fighter." She frowned in the darkness. "Every time I see him, he is clenching his fists."

The heaviness of my spirit lifted as Dawn walked forward and sat next to me on the edge of the cliff. Bear crossed the clearing in five steps, saw the earth plunge toward the lake below, and whimpered, refusing to go any farther.

"Coward." Dawn laughed. "Stay there then, but you're missing an incredible view."

"It isn't easy for Ian."

"I assumed as much."

"How do you do that, Dawn?"

"Do what?"

"Choose the perfect name for people."

The moonlight revealed *Waubun-anung* to me. It glinted off her high cheekbones and shimmered blue on her rippling black hair.

"I guess it runs in my blood. My grandmother was the name giver in our tribe."

"Name giver?"

"The Ojibwe believe that a name captures the spirit of a person, so a name giver is consulted when a child is born. *Gichi-manidoo*, the Great Spirit, gives the perfect name to the name giver in a dream or a vision."

"Are you a name giver too?"

"No, I don't have visions, but sometimes when I'm thinking of a person I hear a name whispered on the wind."

"Who talks to you in the wind? *Gichi-manidoo*?"

"Yes, I believe so."

"But Dawn, aren't you a Christian?" I swallowed hard, not wanting to offend her.

"*Needjee*, does God change just because people call Him by different names?"

"No, I don't suppose so." I thought of all the names for God I had heard growing up in church: God the Father; Jesus Christ, His son; the Holy Spirit; Abba; Yahweh. Why not *Gichi-manidoo* for Dawn and her people? God is God.

"You make it sound so simple." I looked up at the sky and saw constellations of freckles on pale, gleaming skin. Nothing in my life was simple. Not anymore.

"People make things complicated. Not God." Dawn put her hand on my shoulder. A high-pitched shriek broke the quiet of the night. It came from the tree under which Ian and I had shared pie and kisses and fallen asleep in each other's arms. "*Gichi-manidoo* has sent *gookooko'oo* to watch over you tonight."

"*Gookooko'oo*? Oh, you mean the owl? Yeah, he's been talking to me all night." I peered through the darkness, searching the tree, but he stayed hidden. Bear found some courage and inched his way closer to Dawn. He curled his body next to her.

Dawn ran her fingers through his long white fur. "Did you know that owls are important to my people? Some believe that the owl brings a warning that you are surrounded by evil, possibly death. But to others, and I believe this, it is a sign that you will be a great spiritual leader someday. The owl's call still signals a death, but it is your old thoughts that must die in order for *Gichi-manidoo* to give you a new vision and way to believe. My mother would say that your guide has chosen you."

"What would you say?"

"How do I know? The owl brought rescue for *Makwa.* A new life snatched out of the hands of death. I do know that you're not alone. Like *Makwa,* you have a friend watching over you." She stood up. "I'll leave you to your prayers now." Bear jumped to his feet and gave a yip. He bounded ahead of her toward the small opening in the bush, squatted on all fours and army crawled through the opening, his white tail waving good-bye.

Close, so close I could feel his presence, the owl hooted.

Chapter Sixteen

The next morning Ian budged in line for the canteen just so he could talk to me. "What gives? Did I contract the plague and nobody told me?"

"Twizzlers, please." I handed a gold token to Aaron and turned to face Ian. There were words I needed to say to him. Words that sounded like *This has got to stop* in my head.

We walked in awkward silence through the forest. A mouthful of Twizzlers is a great excuse not to talk, by the way. Unfortunately they were gone when we reached Porcupine Point. I strode to the edge of the cliff where I searched for the right words.

"So, spill. What's wrong?" Ian stood next to me. We had a perfect view of camp life: Sara and Sean, in miniature, hung out by the boathouse; tiny Simon painted in the arts-and-crafts pavilion; a small white blur told me Bear was running loose. Again.

The words lodged in my throat. I jammed my hands deep into my pockets and rocked back on my feet.

"Do you suppose this is how God feels when he looks at us? Like, from His perspective we're so busy scurrying around, arguing about the small stuff all the time, that we're missing out on the big picture?" I asked.

"If I believed in God, I suppose that's exactly how I would think he'd feel." Ian crossed his arms in front of his chest.

"What do you mean, *if* you believed in God?"

"I mean I'm not sure what I believe when it comes to God. Why? Is it important to you?"

"Yeah, I guess it is. Are you like an *atheist*?" I turned to look at him. Shocked.

"Relax, Jonathan, you don't go to hell just for saying the word." Ian stepped away from the cliff and sat down on a fallen birch log. "And no, I'm not an atheist. I am not ready to say that there is no God, but if he does exist and he created this world, then I'm not too impressed. So when I say that I don't believe in God, I'm saying that I don't buy the party line."

"What do you mean, the party line?" I swiveled to stare at him.

"You know it better than I do. You sing it and dance it and walk it and talk it. You hallelujah and amen in all the right spots. You know, the party line."

Each word was a punch to the gut. "That's not a party line, Ian. It's what I believe."

"Are you sure?" Ian looked me hard in the eyes.

I shifted my weight. "Of course."

"See, I think you can tell me what you've been told to believe, but I don't think you've ever asked yourself what you do believe. Because I swear, you don't know. I see it whenever you look at me. Whenever you touch me."

"What do you believe then?"

He turned to look at Spirit Lake. "I believe in things I can see. Assholes like Jake, for example. I know they're real. I believe in things that I feel. Like a fist connecting with someone's face, but mostly, I believe in words. No matter what happens, it's always better when I write about it. No matter how much it—"

"Hurts."

"Yeah."

"Is that what you want to be? A writer?" I sat next to him. My head told me to pull away. My heart drew me closer to him.

"Maybe."

"What else do you write besides poetry?"

"Short stories mostly. Then there's this book I'm working on."

"Get out of here! You have got to let me read your book."

Ian looked away. "I don't let people read my writing."

"Not even me?"

"I'll think about it. What about you? Are you going to be a photographer?"

"I doubt it. My dad is third generation career military. He's already talked to a Marine recruiter. Mom wants me to be a youth minister. I guess that'd be okay."

"You know what I think? I think you should be a photographer if that's what you want to be. It's your life."

The words I'd been trying so hard to find slipped away. They floated on the wind. Over the cliff. Into the lake where they sank. "Maybe you could write a book, and I could take the pictures for it."

"The perfect coffee-table book. I can see it now." Ian laughed. "We could call it *A Study of Porcupines, Up Close and Personal* by Ian McGuire."

"With award-winning photography by Jonathan Cooper."

"On clearance for ninety-nine cents at Barnes and Noble!"

"If we're lucky. Probably more like ten cents at Half Price Books." Ian got both of us laughing, and it felt so good. So natural. "Man, I miss bookstores."

The soft wind stirred the trees. Their leaves fluttered and spun, catching the light and revealing the subtle layers of their color. I listened to the soothing sound of Spirit Lake as it rolled against the rocks.

"What's it like, living on a farm?" I asked. Ian and cows just didn't compute.

"It sucks."

"Oh?"

"Yeah, I live in the armpit of Wisconsin in a dinky town where the population scored negative three on the intelligence scale. Everyone there wears Carhartt jackets and hunts. They listen to country music—voluntarily, mind you. It's a joke. They're—"

"Cheeseheads." I laughed.

"Yup, and you know what? I have a serious case of dairy intolerance. For real, man, I hang around those idiots too long, and before you know it I've got the trots. I just want to run and run and run, right out of town."

"What about your family? Wouldn't you miss them?"

"You mean my foster parents."

Foster parents. *I'm nobody's kid.* His words came back to me. Questions I didn't know how to ask ran through my mind.

"I'm sorry."

"For what?"

"For whatever took you away from your parents."

"Don't be. I'm not. My parents emigrated to the Land of the Forever Fucked Up. I'm better off, believe it or not, stuck in Cheeseville than I was before."

I believed him. "I'm still sorry." I placed my hand on Ian's.

"It's just…" He held his breath.

"It's just what?"

"I used to live in Madison. There was a bookstore I loved. I couldn't afford to buy the books, but the lady who owned it let me read for as long as I wanted. I used to lose track of time and get into trouble actually. I miss that bookstore."

I thought about my own parents…my father, George "Butch" Cooper. *That's Gunnery Sergeant Cooper to you, cadet.* Deployed for the third time one month ago. My mother, Linda Cooper, devout Sunday school teacher and maker of hot dinner every night at 1800 hours. My house, the little story-and-a-half bungalow in Minnetonka, white with black shutters and a cranberry door. The first floor belonged to them; the upstairs half story was mine. Half and incomplete. Sure, they'd given me a solid beginning, but an ending I could live with? No, there was no hint of that in my half story with the slanted roof.

I had never felt more privileged or more trapped.

"Was it your foster parents' idea for you to come here?"

"Yeah, I think they're hoping Paul can get through to me. Hell, maybe they just wanted a month without me around. Who knows? I'm not exactly a ray of sunshine back on the farm."

"Maybe the cows complained about you walking around naked all the time," I joked.

He laughed again. "Maybe."

"Hey, you could come and visit me after camp. You know, before school starts or over Christmas break. There are lots of bookstores by me."

"Is there an art gallery?"

"Yeah, there's the Walker Art Center. We could even take in a play at the Guthrie."

"Maybe. We'll see." The breeze picked up and tossed the treetops. "Any more news about your dad?"

"No." I looked away.

"I'm sorry." He read my body language, leaned toward me, eyes half-closed. Mouth so tempting. Moments before his lips touched mine, I remembered the reason I had brought him here.

To end things.

I pulled back and the fragile thing that had grown between us tore.

"I'm sorry, Ian, I…promised Simon I'd help him set up for sculpture class. I gotta go." I jumped to my feet.

"I thought we were going to hang out."

"Yeah, I know, but I promised." I hurried across to the bush with the hidden entrance to Porcupine Point and ducked through the opening.

❖

I walked down the trail, soil and debris littering the path under my feet, and tried to forget how just being around him was enough to prompt a full military salute, so to speak. I stepped out of the forest and into the campground, more confused than ever.

"Oh, hi, Jonathan!"

The voice came from the direction of a huge oak tree next to the arts-and-crafts pavilion. Bethany sat alone under the tree, her *Pass the Pepcid* script in her lap, and waved at me.

"Hey!" I walked over to her. "Studying your lines?"

"Yeah, sort of." She rolled her eyes. "I don't know what to do."

"Having a hard time with the memorization?" I sat down beside her. "Try reading your lines aloud. It helps."

"It's not the memorization that I'm worried about. It's this dance I have to do. It says right here: *Salome dances seductively in front of Herod.*" Bethany's face flushed. She refused to look at me.

"Oh yeah. That is a bit awkward." An image of her full breasts spilling out of her pink bra flashed through my mind. I tried to imagine her dancing seductively. I looked at my crotch. *C'mon!*

Nada. Less than nada.

Zip.

"It's just that my parents will be there. And all my brothers and sisters. And I'm supposed to, well, dance seductively in front of you!" Bethany looked frantic.

"Don't worry. It's going to be okay."

Bethany leaned her head against my shoulder. I remembered the last time I'd spoken those words to her and the kiss that had followed.

Still nothing.

"I'm sure you're right." She slipped her hand into mine. "I'll just keep my eyes on you the whole time. That'll be easy to do."

Small and smooth, so easy to hold, her hand fit perfectly into my hand. The sweet scent of the coconuts surrounded me. My stomach rolled. Not exactly the physical reaction I'd been hoping for. I stood and let Bethany's hand slide out of mine.

"I'm sorry, Bethany, I've got to go." I walked away and didn't look back.

I am not gay! Ian's laugh, the one that came out like a snort and meant *bullshit*, echoed in my head.

I couldn't argue with him.

Miserable, I headed to my cabin. I needed to be alone.

CHAPTER SEVENTEEN

Sunday morning dawned, and the whole camp gathered for Songs by the Shore. Aaron sat cross-legged in the shadow of the Cyprus cross, his guitar propped on his right knee. He hung his head forward as if he was straining to hear the music his guitar wanted to create. He played, slow and soft at first, matching the tempo of the waves. Without warning he jerked his shoulders and began to pick. Lightning quick. A duet, a trio, an entire choir erupted from his guitar. Aaron swayed back and forth, left and right, a slight smile playing over his lips. He was immersed in the music. I was too. The last note hung in the air, dying into silence.

Paul began speaking as the long, graceful branches of the willow tree cascaded into the backdrop behind him. "I thought today we would talk about a tough subject. It's one that no one ever wants to tackle head-on, and yet it's a subject we all wrestle with in our lives." He paused. "Our subject today is temptation. Let's begin by talking about the things we find tempting."

"I almost cheated on a biology test last year," Bryan admitted. "But I didn't. I just felt tempted."

"I can never turn down chocolate," Lily confessed.

Pretty tame stuff, in my opinion. I glanced at Jake, remembering the porn magazines, but he stared straight ahead. For one crazy moment I heard a voice in my mind urging me to speak up. Then I imagined the chaos that would follow. I looked at Ian and felt my stomach lurch.

"Temptation is a tough thing, kids. It comes in many forms as we've just learned, but all temptation comes from Satan whose primary goal is to drive a wedge between God and us. One of the most powerful temptations is sex. Yes, that's right. I said the word and we all survived." Paul chuckled at our shocked faces. "Why am I telling you this? Because it's the truth and you need to hear it now, more than ever. Your bodies are not doing you any favors right now in this battle between God and Satan. Adolescent hormones create feelings that are new and confusing and powerful. God calls us to purity. He asks that we save ourselves until the day when we have entered into a sacred covenant with the person He has chosen to be our mate. On that day He will bless our union and all these feelings will become incredible gifts given to us by God. But make no mistake about this: giving in to temptation has the power to turn one of God's greatest blessings in our lives into a curse."

The scent of Hannah's Sunday morning brunch reached the lakeshore. Paul dismissed us with his standard phrase, *Go in peace and serve the Lord.* I sat by the shore, long after everyone had left, and prayed for answers, but all I heard was the lazy lapping of the water against the rocks. Finally I gave up and walked toward the dining hall where I knew both Ian and Bethany would be saving a seat for me. Though everything about me grumbled, especially my stomach, I had no appetite.

After a lazy Sunday afternoon, Aaron announced that we were getting together with the other guys' cabins down at the fire pit. Ian, of course, managed to sit right next to me, his body pressing against mine.

"Welcome!" Sean projected over the rumble of voices while Aaron and Simon passed out hot dogs and whittled twigs. "We know Paul gave you a lot to think about today during his purity talk. We thought it would be fun have some guy time, pig out, and then discuss any questions you might have. But first, let's eat."

"Is this how you do it?" Ian plunged a hot dog on a stick into the fire. The flesh blackened and burst.

"No, not exactly."

I laughed as Ian scowled at his charred hot dog. The constant tension that played itself out like a yo-yo, half the time drawing me to him and half the time pushing me away from him, eased as we laughed together. "See, watch. You've got to hold it close to the heat, but don't put it in the fire. Unless you like cremated meat by-products." I turned my stick and rotated the hot dog inches away from the direct flame until it browned.

"Not so much." Ian sniffed his burned-beyond-salvation hot dog. "What do I do with this?"

"Give it to me. I don't care if it's burned," Jake said. "I'll eat it." Ian handed him the stick with the charred remains. I gave Ian my hot dog and impaled another on my stick while he tore open the package of buns.

"Mmmm, good. Can you make me another?" Ian tried to smile, but it didn't work too well with his mouth full.

"Nope, you've got to learn for yourself. Somehow, I think you can handle it. After that I'll show you how to roast a marshmallow. Same principle, but a bit trickier." I grinned, betting Hannah had also provided dessert.

"Wonderful." I had no clue whether Ian was complimenting my outdoor cooking skills or complaining because I was refusing to wait on him. Knowing him, probably both.

❖

"So, I'm a big fan of s'mores, but I don't think I can eat another. I'm stuffed." Ian wiped the melted chocolate from his lips. He stretched toward the fire that had settled into a smoldering glow and inhaled the heady scent of smoke. His shoulders, usually so tight, relaxed, and for the first time since I'd known him, he looked happy.

Sean stood and clapped his hands to get our attention. "Okay, guys, everyone done eating?" He looked around the circle. "Great! Aaron, Simon, and I wanted to get our cabins together so we could talk about the things that are important to you. Before we begin though, let's invite God into this discussion. Simon, would you lead us in prayer?"

"Glad to." Simon bowed his head, and I followed his example. "Father, thank You for blessing Aaron, Sean, and me with the privilege of spending four weeks with these awesome young men. Thank You for this place that is so filled with exquisite examples of Your tremendous love for us. We are humbled. We pray that You use this time in a special way. Amen."

"Thank you, Simon," Sean continued. "We're going to start with some questions, just to get our conversation going. Please speak up. So, first of all: How did you feel about Paul's talk today? Any thoughts?"

No one wanted to speak first. I looked at the three-quarter moon that hung over us, reflecting the sun's light from the other side of the earth. Nearly full-grown. So close.

I shattered the awkward silence. "I think Paul wanted us to know that there are some things we may think we're ready to experience, but we aren't. Like sex."

"That's good, Jonathan. Any other thoughts about Paul's talk? Now's the time to be honest, guys. We'll tell it to you straight," Simon said.

"It was lame." Jake threw a twig in the fire. "No sex before marriage. Like that's a song and dance none of us have ever heard before. You know what I wanted to hear him talk about? Guys doing guys and chicks doing chicks. I wanted to hear Paul tell us what he thinks about that."

Me too, I thought.

"Actually, you bring up an important issue." Aaron nodded at Jake. "Homosexuality is a tough question for believers right now. Churches are being ripped apart by it. The Bible is clear about homosexuality, but our society tells us something quite different. What do you guys think?"

"God made Adam and Eve. Not Adam and Steve," Jake said. "I had a new English teacher last year and he was cool, you know? He let us choose where we sat and he talked to us different than the other a-holes we got for teachers. Most of the time school sucks, but his class was all right. At least I stayed awake. Then I hear he's banging a dude. I mean, gross. If Paul's going to talk about sex and all, I just think he should talk about that too."

"What do the rest of you think?" Aaron asked.

"My mom says we should pray for gay people. She says that the Bible calls homosexuality an abomination. I looked it up and she was right," Bryan said. "I think that means they're damned. So we need to pray for them."

Simon scowled into the fire. He opened his mouth to speak, but Aaron beat him to the punch.

"Your mom is absolutely right. The Bible does say that when a man lies with a man as he lies with a woman it is an abomination. It's in Leviticus. But the Bible is talking about the act. Like any other sin, if a person truly is repentant, God will forgive and heal. It is the people who do not repent who risk damnation. That's why we need to love people who are in bondage to sin and especially to this lifestyle. We are not to bully them or hate them. Rather, we are to shine God's love into their lives and pray for them. You've heard the phrase *Hate the sin and love the sinner,* right?" Aaron asked. "That goes double for homosexuals."

I shifted my weight and stared into the fire.

"What gives you people the right to judge?" Ian's shoulders were hard and tight again.

Simon leaned forward in his wheelchair, preparing to answer him, but then Ian stood up abruptly.

"Ian, please sit down. I think you have something important to contribute to this discussion."

"Not likely." He stalked off.

It's okay. Let him go. Simon mouthed the words to me. I couldn't concentrate after that. My mind kept returning to Ian and the fire in his eyes, the anger in his shoulders.

Back at the cabin, while Bryan fried more mosquitoes, Jake and Aaron continued talking about God's condemnation of homosexuality.

"What you need to understand, Jake, is that Satan is devious. He preys on the unnatural desires of the flesh to separate people from God."

My ears filled with a buzzing sound. I sprang out of my bunk, sick of the whole damn thing, and grabbed my camera and a flashlight.

"Hey, Aaron, is it okay if I take some night pictures?" I stood at the door, determined to walk out regardless of his answer.

"Yeah, sure. Just be back before it's too late. I need to know everyone is safe before I zonk out."

"Understood." Outside, the night hummed with a richness of life I'd only found along the North Shore and never anywhere stronger than at Spirit Lake. The air teased my skin, tickling one spot and then another. It ruffled my hair. My head began to clear. Light from the moon broke through the leaves overhead, sending down a dozen or so patches of light around me.

I wandered from illuminated scene to scene, peering through my camera lens. A ladybug crawled on a leaf. Cool. But not right for black-and-white shots. I stepped out of the forest and into the campground. The moon was throwing one heck of a party and all the big stars had made an appearance: Cassiopeia, Big Dipper, Little Dipper, Orion, even the North Star. That view tied for first place with the scent of the wind in the category of Things I Love Best About Northern Minnesota. In the distance, the crickets called me. I walked forward, camera still in hand, studying the moonlight and the way it changed everything. Suddenly the perfect black-and-white shot appeared.

I ran my hand over the scar on the smooth, gleaming skin of the birch tree. There was a story there.

The light was tricky. I set my Nikon to manual mode and my shutter speed to thirty seconds. Kneeling on the ground, I made a tripod by resting my elbow on my knee. I zoomed in until the whole frame filled with the scarred skin. Click.

I walked until I stood about thirty feet away from Spirit Lake and looked at the peaceful beach. The waves massaged the shore, smoothing over the broken surface of a hard day.. I zoomed way out to see the whole beach. The dark sand and the lake that shone white with the moon's reflection filled the frame. Click. No particular story, just a picture of a place I loved.

"What gives you the right to judge?" A voice shattered the moment and drew my attention to someone standing on the beach. I walked toward him and then froze. Anger rippled off him as he kicked the Cyprus cross where we gathered for Songs by the Shore. His feet struck it over and over again. "Pray the gay away, my ass!"

I stood, unable to take in the scene in front of me.

"What are you doing?" I shouted.

"Get out of here, Jonathan! This doesn't have anything to do with you!"

"Like hell it doesn't, Ian."

He swiveled toward me. The wail of a loon broke through the night. Probably Edward. From far across the lake, Bella answered. I read hesitation in his eyes.

"Ian, this thing between us, it's wrong. We've got to put an end to this. You heard what the Bible says—"

"That's why you've been avoiding me?" Fresh anger erupted on his face. "Because of your God?" He growled. He hurled one last desperate kick. Deep indentations showed along the soft wood where his feet had assaulted the cross. He sank to the ground and sat on the sand. He turned his face toward the lake and refused to look at me. He raised his hand as if to wipe away tears. Edward and Bella wailed again across the lake, still lost, still searching for each other. I sat next to him on the damp sand.

"You want to end it?" he asked. "Fine. Fuck it. It's over."

"I still want to be your friend." I leaned toward him. Close enough that our arms touched, and held up my camera. "'Cause I'm better with a lens. Remember?"

"We were never friends." He looked at me, the anger having drained from his face. Only the pain remained.

I looked at the cross and then at Ian. The damage that had been done could not be undone. Each bore the scars, but Ian's were written on his heart and in his eyes.

"I thought I could handle it, the way you hide behind a faith that doesn't want anything to do with the real you. But I can't. Know why? Because you're hiding even from yourself. You're just as angry as I am. You're just not as honest." Ian took one long look at me and walked away.

The camera felt heavy in my hands. Like a friendship that was too hard to bear. I hit the review button and zoomed in on the last shot, the full beach scene. There, in perfect-silhouetted clarity, I'd captured Ian: face contorted in anger…foot striking the cross. My hand trembled as I pressed the delete button.

Erase image? Yes or No? the camera asked. My chest tightened. It was a fair question. The default answer was no. *Keep this image,* it argued. *It's proof.*

The other choice was yes. *Delete this image and protect him. He has a right to be angry,* it argued. *So do you.*

A fair question. Just not an easy one.

CHAPTER EIGHTEEN

The light from my camera shone in the darkness of my bunk. I stared at the image of Ian, foot striking the cross. Rage, recorded in 1600 pixels. *Was I angry too?* His question kept me awake. *Abomination. Pray the gay away. Adam and Eve, not Adam and Steve.* The phrases echoed in my mind, dredging up feelings that transported me to a day two years ago.

My father had returned from his second tour of duty. I was fourteen and everything about me was a hand grenade with the pin pulled but the trigger still held tight. Waiting for the hormones to explode.

He had come home…different. Quieter. He couldn't stand loud noises so I mastered the art of tiptoeing through the house. Heel to toe. Heel to toe. In stealth mode. *We need to pray for him,* my mother had told me, and I had. Every morning and every night and a dozen times in between.

It was July 4th, two years ago, the night before I went to camp. The air in the living room was heavy and damp. The wobbling ceiling fan managed a weak breeze; its constant whine grated against my nerves. My father sat in his La-Z-Boy. I crashed on the floor, elbow leaning on the coffee table's veneer surface, and studied the deep lines of his face, looking for answers. My mother curled up on the couch, knitting.

It was a blistering summer.

Hot.

"Iraq hot?" I'd asked my father.

"Not even close." His hand ran across my crew cut, long and starting to wilt. "You need a buzz cut before you go to camp. Otherwise, you might get put in a girls' cabin by mistake." He took a sip of coffee and scalded his lips. "Damn it!"

"Iraq hot?" I asked again.

"Almost, but no. Not quite."

Instead of going into the bathroom to get the hair clippers, he reached for the TV remote. Seventeen hundred hours: time for the news. Video of a protest in Washington, DC flashed across the screen. People carried signs. A man with long hair, wearing a rainbow pin with *DADT* crossed out, shouted at the reporter:

Our country is falling apart. Unemployment has skyrocketed. The housing market has plummeted. Yet how is this administration spending our tax dollars? On a pointless war we have no business fighting! By sending our kids into the Middle East where they're good enough to die as long as they don't talk about their sexual orientation. End the war in the Middle East! End Don't Ask, Don't Tell *now!*

The television went blank. My father scowled as he slammed the remote down.

"I'd like to see that guy face down enemy fire. He'd probably crap his pants." The tone of his voice was hot.

Iraq hot.

I was sure of it.

My mom looked up from her knitting. "They don't understand, sweetheart. They don't know what it's like."

"What's *Don't Ask, Don't Tell*?" I asked.

"It's the military's policy about gay soldiers," my father said, using the same tone to explain his view of sexuality that he used when he explained geometry to me. Matter of fact. Rectangles—right angled and sturdy. Ninety degrees of masculinity. Circles—rounded and gentle. Full of feminine curves. What about the not so easy to define isosceles triangles and parallelograms?

Don't ask, don't tell.

The Pentagon didn't want to know.

I thought of my new book, hidden between the mattress and box spring of my bed. *Boy Meets Boy* by David Levithan. I'd stumbled across it at the Barnes & Noble and bought it with the gift card Grandma had given me for Christmas. I'd crumpled up the receipt and thrown it away at the store. No proof. A good covert mission depends on leaving no evidence.

"What's the big deal if a gay person is in the military? I don't get it."

"Jon, imagine that you're in a war. Fighting an enemy. Putting your life on the line. Day after day. You have to know you can trust the people in your platoon, right? Your life depends on it."

"Okay. Sure."

"Allow an openly gay person in a military unit and pretty soon you've got guys who are convinced he's checking them out in the shower. It"—he searched for the right word—"unsettles everyone. Gays can serve. That's fine. I just don't want to know about it. So we don't ask and they don't tell. Trust me, Jon, it's best for everyone, including them."

"And you know what the Bible says about homosexuality." My mother's knitting needles clicked in perfect rhythm, pulling thread from the wicker basket that sat at her feet. A rainbow of yarn, balled up within, waited to unravel.

Later, when the house filled with the sounds of pans clanking in the kitchen and the droning of the history channel in the living room, I snuck into their bathroom, took the hair clippers, and headed into the garage. Hot, maybe not Iraq hot, but damned close. Sweating from the stifling air that pressed down on me and choking from the scent of gasoline and oil that burned my nose, I flung the clippers on the hard cement floor. The shattered pieces, none of them perfect rectangles or circles, flew in every direction.

❖

I peered through the darkness of the cabin and looked again at the image of Ian, honest in his anger. And what about me? Was I angry too?

Erase image? Yes or No? the camera asked again. I hit the upward button and highlighted the word *Yes* and pressed the button. The picture vanished.

Hell, yes. I was angry.

Chapter Nineteen

For days I waited for Paul to demand answers about the defiled cross, but he never said a word. His eyes lingered just a little longer on Ian than before. The glances he gave me asked unspoken questions, but I followed my father's boot steps. If Paul didn't ask, I wasn't going to tell.

Almost everyone hit the lake early on Monday morning, as the last week of camp began. It was a perfect morning for Paul's annual five-loaves-and-two-fish competition, which always culminated in a gut-busting fish fry. It was a day the rest of the camp looked forward to and I always dreaded.

Worms were impaled. Fish suffocated. All around me, people celebrated death. So while the anglers hit the lake, Ian—who declared the event barbaric—and I stayed behind with Simon, who maintained that wheelchairs and fishing boats were not compatible. Bear sat next to me, watching Dawn, who stood, thigh deep, in the lake. She held a long spear in her hand. Bent in full concentration, she stared at the world that teemed with life beneath the surface. A woven basket hung from a strap around her shoulder. She stood, still as one of Simon's statues, until she plunged her spear into the lake. She struck like lightning and withdrew her spear, an impaled fish wriggling on it. Dawn removed the fish and held it in her hands. Her rich, deep voice, chanting in Ojibwe, carried over the water to Simon and me. The only word I understood was *miigwech*, which I knew meant thank-you. Her hands were merciful. One quick snap and its suffering ended.

"What did she say?" I turned to Simon who followed Dawn's every movement. "Do you know?"

"She told me once that it is the way of her people to thank the Great Spirit for providing for their needs as well as to thank the fish for making the ultimate sacrifice. I imagine that's what she's saying. She'll never take more fish than she needs for the day, and she'll use every last bit of the fish. She'll fillet the meat and make fish soup with the head and skin."

Jake hollered across the lake, holding a huge fish over his head like a trophy on display. Landed a big one, I supposed. "We could learn a lot from the Ojibwe," I said.

"We sure could."

My eyes strayed to Ian, who sat under the willow tree, writing in his journal. "Hey, Simon, can I ask you something personal?"

"What do you want to know?" Simon smiled as Dawn took up her statue stance again.

"Have you ever been in love?"

Simon jerked his face toward me. "Come again?"

"Sorry. You don't have to answer." I stared at the willow tree.

"No, it's okay. You just surprised me. Yes, I know what it's like to be in love. Why do you ask?"

"I was just curious. How do you know it's love and not something else?" Simon followed my glance. Out of the corner of my eye I saw him nod and smile as if he'd just figured something out.

"That's easy. I knew I was in love because I couldn't make a sentence come out right whenever I talked to her. I had a bad case of verbal dyslexia."

"Smooth, Simon!" I laughed with him. "What happened when you told her?"

"I'll let you know when I do." He grinned.

"What do you mean? You haven't told her?" Simon's words stunned me.

"Nope."

"Why not?"

"It's complicated."

Tell me about it. "What's holding you back from telling her?" I probed.

"She's…active." Simon's eyes fell to his chair. "I have to think about what she'd be giving up to be with me. I have to think about what's best for her. I still haven't decided. Now, how about you, Casanova? Why are you asking about love?"

"Last night at the bonfire…what we talked about—you know, God and sinners? Well, the more I thought about that, the more confused I got. I didn't know who I could talk to."

"I'm glad you came to me." Simon glanced at the battered cross. "Let me say this: I don't agree with the position Aaron took at the bonfire."

"You don't? But the Bible says—"

"Listen, this world is pretty tough on gay people. They are teased, bullied, and discriminated against. Why would a person choose such a hard life?"

"So you think a person is born gay."

"I think we are born exactly as God created us to be."

That stunned me. I had never heard a Christian speak like that before. "But you're here at Spirit Lake Bible Camp, with Paul and Aaron and all the rest. I mean, I don't get it."

"I am with God, Jonathan. First and foremost, I am with God, and He sent me here with work to do. Sure, I knew the beliefs of the people here and, strange as this might sound, I've grown to respect them over the years for their authenticity. It's true I disagree with some of their beliefs, but I can't fault them with hypocrisy."

"But the Bible calls homosexuality an abomination!"

"We can talk about that later, but first I want you to read 1 and 2 Samuel. Research another young man named Jonathan and his most precious relationship. Then come talk to me again. In the meantime—"

"I know, this is between us, right?"

"Wrong. I have said nothing to you today that I wouldn't say to anyone else here. Secrets are crippling, and I'm no cripple." Simon slapped the arm of his wheelchair and grinned. "I was going to tell you to pray in the meantime. This is between you and God. Tell Him everything you want to say. Ask any question you need answered. You know all those pretty prayers you've learned? Scrap them and just talk to God. He can handle you being angry or confused. He already knows what you're feeling anyway, and He wants to help you with this. Believe me, I know."

"What do you mean, you know?"

Simon grew still. His animated face quieted into a still mask.

"I don't usually talk about this, but I think you may need to hear my story. When I was fifteen years old, a bit younger than you, I took my dad's car out for a ride. I wasn't supposed to. I only had my permit, but I told myself it was no big deal. I'd have my license in two weeks when I turned sixteen. Anyway, I hit a patch of ice and I didn't know what to do. The car spun out of control. I remember screaming and seeing the tree out of the corner of my eye and then nothing until I woke up in the hospital, unable to move or feel anything from my chest down."

Simon stared beyond me, his eyes, unfocused, seeing something far, far away. I held my breath and waited for him to tell me more.

"I got the use of my arms back eventually. My family and friends threw a party." Simon frowned as the memory played out in his mind. "I told them to take their goddamned cake and shove it up their asses. Then I told God that if His idea of fair punishment for borrowing the car was to take away my legs, then He could go to Hell and rot there. I didn't give a damn as long as He left me alone for the rest of my miserable life." Simon's forehead glistened.

"You don't have to tell me any more," I whispered.

"No, I do because what happened next is the important part. I was sixteen years old and a paraplegic. Every dream I'd had in my life had vanished because of one stupid, impulsive decision. I was miserable and miserable to be around for a long time. I screamed at everyone: my parents, my friends, even the hospital staff that tried to help me, but no one got it worse than God. Day after day I unloaded my fury on Him. One day He talked back."

"What do you mean talked back? You hear God talk?"

"He speaks to me here when I get out of the way enough to listen." Simon put his hand over his heart, and I knew what he meant. "One day, when I was trying to think of a way to end it all, I suddenly felt an electric presence in my room. A warm tingling moved through me, even into my legs, filling me with the presence of God. He told me that my life wasn't over just because I was paralyzed and angry and depressed. That dark day in the hospital, God showed me how He sees me and how much He loves me, and I've never been able to shake that vision. He planted it deep inside me along with the knowledge that His love is unconditional for all of us."

The boats turned and headed for the shore. I rose, not wanting anyone else to overhear this conversation. "For all of us, Simon? Really?"

"Absolutely. Unconditional love for every single person on this planet. That's God's specialty. So talk to Him. Tell Him everything you're feeling. After you've prayed, take time to listen with your heart. God is still speaking to us. We just need to have ears to hear Him."

"Thanks for telling me about what happened to you." I smiled. The sound of splashing drew our attention back to the lake.

"Looks like it's lunchtime." Simon turned to look at Dawn as she walked toward us, the bright sunlight gleaming on her strong arms and legs. The woven basket hung from her shoulder, lower than before.

Sacrifices had been made.

"Hungry, gentlemen? *Makwa?*" Bear, who had been jumping on his back legs and snapping at a butterfly that hovered just beyond his reach, dropped to all fours and ran to greet Dawn, his butt wiggling with delight. "*Gichi-manidoo* was generous today. *Bi-wiisinin*—let's eat!"

Thanks had been given.

"Ian, get your nose out of that book and come join us," Simon hollered. "Lunch is on Dawn." The lines of his face softened as he said her name, and I knew.

Secrets had been exchanged.

Later that night in the pitch-black of the cabin, I read my Bible by flashlight. My head spun as I learned about Jonathan and David, two men whose lives were transformed by their love for each other. Jonathan, the beloved son and rightful heir to King Saul's throne. David, the scrappy fighter who faced a giant with a slingshot and a small, rounded rock. Jonathan, the boy who risked even his relationship with his father because of his love for David. David, the talented musician and writer. Jonathan, loyal and loving to the end…my namesake. David, the boy who became the greatest king of Israel.

I took my father's picture out from between the sheets of my Bible where I kept him safe, the desert sand swirling behind him. I whispered to him in the darkness, "King David, Dad, a great soldier and a man after God's own heart. Think about that."

My father remained unimpressed. He continued to smile at me, confident and covered in impenetrable Kevlar. I tucked the picture back into the soft pages, clicked off my flashlight, and slid my Bible beneath my pillow. *WWJD?* I stared at the insistent letters, carved deep into the bunk above me, and searched for an answer as I drifted off into a troubled sleep, listening to the whine of doomed mosquitoes and the *zzzt* of their electrocution.

Chapter Twenty

"Wow, I can't believe you beat me to rehearsal." Ian swung his leg over the bench and looked at me from across the table in the empty dining room. "I thought you weren't a morning person."

The sound of clattering pans confirmed Hannah's presence in the back kitchen. The aroma of French toast and maple syrup seeped through the empty dining hall.

"I was hoping for a chance to talk to you before the others get here. About the night at the cross."

"There isn't anything more to talk about. You made yourself clear. We're friends and in a few days we'll go back to our homes and that'll be that."

"No, I mean, yeah, we are friends, but that's *not* that. You said I was hiding. Remember?"

"Yeah."

"I've been thinking…"

"And?"

"And I don't want to hide anymore. Not from myself." The words rushed out of my mouth like a speeding train from a tunnel. "And not from you."

Ian raised an eyebrow and looked at me. "What exactly does that mean?"

"It means that every second of my day is measured by you. Do you know that? It's not ten a.m. anymore. It's two hours until lunch. Maybe I'll see Ian there. It's not nine a.m. It's half an hour until sculpture class. I wonder if he'll sit by me. The highlight of my day is Curtain Call because I know I'll hear your voice, even if you're just reciting lines."

I hung my head as if the gravity of my confession pulled me toward Earth and away from Heaven, but there was no going back.

"I believe in Jesus, Ian. I do. But I don't have any answers when it comes to this feeling I get whenever I'm around you. It doesn't make any sense. It doesn't fit with anything I've been taught." I raked my fingers through my hair, praying he would say something, anything that told me he understood.

"Okay, as long as we're being honest, you should know I've been thinking a lot too."

Ian turned his notebook over and over in his hands. Finally he placed it on the table in front of him and pushed it across to me.

"Here." He drew his hands back across the table and put them in his lap.

"You're letting me read this? *Really?*"

"Yeah, I guess I am. You'll be the first person other than me to read it."

"Cool!" I flipped through the notebook. My eyes fell on a poem he had titled "Your fingers brush the lily pad."

My idea of the perfect day:
80 degrees,
light breeze.
Our canoe slices Spirit Lake.
One look at you and I feel myself quake.

My hands shook. The poem took up the whole page, but the words blurred and I couldn't keep reading. I took his thin, freckled hands in mine and stared at his jagged, uneven fingernails.

"I know exactly how I'm going to play Herodias." MacKenzie's voice traveled through the screen window. We pulled apart just as she walked into the dining hall with Bethany, Lily, and Kari.

"Hey, Bethany, wait up." Jake sprinted after them, but Bethany ignored him.

"Hi, Jonathan." She spotted me. Hannah walked in carrying a tray of syrup jugs.

"Good morning, everyone," Sara sang out as she entered the dining hall. "Everyone, gather up. Today we're going to practice a few crucial scenes before breakfast. Only three days until showtime!"

I looked down at Ian's notebook, then back at him and raised an eyebrow.

You keep it. Ian mouthed the words. *It's okay.*

"We're going to practice the dance today." Bethany approached our table. Her face flushed a deep shade of crimson.

"Don't worry. You're going to be fine." I stood up and set the notebook on the floor next to my jacket.

"Jonathan and Bethany, we need to practice that dance scene." Sara snapped her fingers. "Ian, Simon asked if you could run over to the arts-and-crafts pavilion for a second. He's working on the bust of your head. Kari, Lily, and MacKenzie, could you check in with Hannah about the food for the dinner scene? Jake, could you move a few of these tables against the wall? We're going to practice the main dinner scene again once everyone gets back. It's getting down to the wire, kids. We need to get all the details worked out now."

Time to practice being seduced. Ugh. I stole a quick glance behind me as I trailed after Bethany just in time to see Jake lean his weight into a table and give it a shove. It skidded across the room and banged against the wall where my jacket lay on the floor.

❖

"It was right here, Ian! I swear it was!" The rest of the cast had left. The dining hall was empty, except for Ian and me.

I spun in a circle, searching every corner of the room. "I don't understand. Where could it be?" I walked to my jacket that lay on the floor and picked it up for the hundredth time.

"I'd say it's obvious. Jake took it." Ian's face was unreadable.

"Why? Why would he take your notebook?"

"Because he's a major douche nozzle. Guys like that don't need a reason."

"Maybe someone picked it up by accident. It's possible." Just not likely. "Ian, I…you trusted me, and I lost your notebook." I couldn't look him in the eyes.

"Stop beating yourself up. We both know you didn't lose it."

The notebook still had not reappeared as we sat on the dock with our jeans rolled up, feet dangling into the cool water, and watched the sun sizzle into the lake. Silent and stone-faced, Ian stared at the horizon. I had run out of apologies and was wallowing in guilt when I heard the smack of flip-flops behind me. I looked toward the sound and saw Bethany walking down the dock toward us, her long hair loose and swaying.

"Hi, Jonathan!" She waved. "Oh, and hi, Ian. The counselors are having their staff meeting with Paul tonight. A couple of us are getting a bonfire going. C'mon, it'll be much more fun with you there." She stared at me.

"What do you say, Ian?" I bumped shoulders with him. He blinked and surfaced from the stupor.

"Yeah, sure. Bonfire, whatever."

We got up, unrolled our jeans, put our shoes on, and followed Bethany toward the bonfire. The heat from the five-foot-tall flames hit me full force as I walked up and found Bryan pouring something from a bottle into a clear plastic cup.

"What happens at camp, stays at camp." He handed a glass to each of us. "On threat of retaliation. Epic retaliation. Understand, Cooper?"

I glanced at the bottle. Manischewitz concord grape. The kind my mom drank because it was holy. "You raided Paul's communion wine? What? How?"

Bryan laughed. "They don't lock anything up around here. I swear I waltzed right into the kitchen and helped myself. Seriously, it was that easy."

"Oh, I believe you," I said, glancing sideways at Ian.

Bethany looked at her glass like she was expecting Satan to jump out and poke her with his pitchfork. Ian, however, drained his in one gulp and muttered, "Why couldn't they have served beer at the Last Supper?"

And me? I did what I always do whenever I'm in this circumstance. I walked over to the bonfire and sat down, the glass in my hand. I learned a few years ago at the end of season soccer party that I don't actually have to drink. I just have to carry a glass around.

Bethany sipped her wine and sat down next to me on my right. Ian said something indistinguishable and most likely profane under his breath and sat to my left.

"Mom would go ballistic if she knew I was drinking." Bethany took another sip.

I considered telling her that two sips hardly qualified as drinking, but then she took a third. And a fourth. And before I knew it, her glass was empty and she had propped her legs on top of mine and was leaning toward me, giving me a clear shot down her shirt. Who knew I'd miss the sight of a bra? I tried to scoot closer to Ian, but he was sending death rays out of his eyes at Jake who seemed oblivious to the danger he was in. Which reminded me.

"Hey, Bethany, you didn't happen to see anyone pick up Ian's journal at Curtain Call this morning, did you?" The wind shifted direction, blowing the smoke away. The scent of her perfume assaulted me.

"You mean that notebook he's always writing in? No. Why?" She held her glass out to Bryan who was making the rounds with another bottle of contraband communion wine.

He spotted my full glass. "Dude, drink up. Looks like you're in for an epic night." He winked at me, and I imagined frying him with his stupid mosquito zapper.

Ian exhaled. "August. Imperial. Magnificent. Splendid. There are more synonyms for the word epic, Bryan, but that's a start."

Bryan frowned as he walked away. "What's his problem?"

Beside me, Ian ran out of words and resorted to groaning.

Jake got up and high-stepped over the sprawling limbs of couples who were well on their way to making lilac, if not purple, until he reached us and sat down next to Bethany.

"H-hey," he stuttered, "I was wondering if you'd like to go for a walk in the forest. You know, with me." He looked toward the edge of the trees and grinned…if groveling and grinning were synonyms, that is.

"Thanks, but Jonathan and I were talking about something Ian lost at Curtain Call this morning." Bethany rested her hand on my leg. "A notebook."

Beside me, Ian stiffened.

Jake frowned and stood up. "Jonathan and you, huh? Having a nice little talk about Ian's notebook? This notebook?" He pulled something from his back pocket.

"Hey everybody. Listen to this." Jake opened the notebook. "*I nearly told him today. I found myself thinking that I could be happy just sitting with him on this log being a blood donor for mosquitoes for the rest of my life. I can't decide if I'm relieved or sad that I said nothing. What if I told him and he didn't feel the same way, isn't the same way? But if he did, if he was? Oh God, he's all I can think about.* Looks like Ian's in *love*."

Jake made the word sound smutty.

Oh shit! Giggles and whispers blew around the bonfire. Ian stumbled to his feet and moved away from the circle.

Jake called out after him. "This is your notebook, isn't it?"

Ian broke into a full run toward the woods.

"Where are you going? You haven't told us who Lover Boy is. Not that we all can't guess! Okay, you must not care about this then." Jake tossed the notebook into the bonfire.

"No!" I dropped my glass of wine and lunged for the notebook.

It didn't matter that I burned my hands.

It didn't matter that MacKenzie's mouth fell open.

It didn't even matter that Bethany lost her balance and fell off the log when I sprang to my feet.

Only two things mattered: saving Ian's journal and getting to him as fast as possible.

I knew exactly where to go.

I shoved the journal into my back pocket and ran into the woods where I found him, sitting on a fallen birch log at Porcupine Point, his small frame shaking and curved in on itself.

"Ian, are you okay?" I took a step toward him. He stiffened at the sound of my voice.

"Yeah." He jerked his head away.

"You sure?" I took a few more steps toward him.

He turned to look at me. His eyes, wild with pain, penetrated me.

"No, I'm not okay. I'm not okay at all." His voice shook.

I sat next to him on the log and looked at Spirit Lake. A river of light shimmered where the moon touched the water. "Hey, it's going to be okay. Really." I laid a hand on his shoulder.

He snapped his shoulder and flung my hand away. He stood up. His hands, clenched at his sides, formed fists. He paced in front of me. "I swore I'd never let anyone do that to me again! Make me feel small and vulnerable and ashamed!"

Ian put his hand in his pocket and took out his straight razor.

"What are you doing? Give me the razor." I stood up and looked him in the eye. Held my hand out to him.

"Compact, smooth and polished on the outside. Impressive, right?"

"Yeah."

"It's just like him, you know. This is all I have left of him. My dad washed out of boot camp, but he ran our home like it was one."

At least the perfect military salute made sense now.

"Ian, I'm not kidding. I don't give a shit about your dad. I give a shit about you. Now give me the goddamned razor." My voice was steel.

"Jonathan Cooper, junior counselor wannabe, I am a bad influence on you, aren't I?" He flipped his wrist. The blade flashed in the moonlight. "It took less than that to find my dad's dangerous side. I don't even know why I still carry this damned thing around with me."

Ian walked to the edge of the cliff, talking to Spirit Lake. Or the stars that hung over our heads. Or to the birds that chattered in the nearby trees. Or the jagged rocks below.

"He caught me looking at a website. I told him it was a mistake…that I'd clicked on it by accident. He didn't believe me. When he finished with me, I was more black-and-blue than white. That's when they took me."

"Took you? Who took you?" I asked his back, uncertain if he was even listening to me anymore.

"The sheriff with his badge and the social worker with her court papers. You know what's fucked up? My parents didn't even say good-bye."

I couldn't see his face, but I heard the sound of tears in his voice. I wanted to go to him, but fear of what he might do had superglued my feet to the ground and my mouth shut.

"She looked at me like I was a stranger." Ian's voice broke. "I kept saying over and over, Mom, it's still me. I'm still the same. What does it matter that when I look at a boy I feel something? What's the big fucking deal?" He snapped the razor shut. "She never did answer my question. She just watched as the sheriff put me in the backseat of the squad car, like I was the fucking criminal."

Ian wound his arm back and pitched the razor over the cliff. I heard it smash and imagined it shattering into a thousand little pieces on the rocks below. He turned around to face me. The glow of the moon behind him cast a shadow that fell across his face. He was past talking. He was shouting.

"Like I said, my parents emigrated to the Land of the Forever Fucked Up. Screw 'em. And screw Paul and Jake and all the other people here and their bullshit phrases like *Hate the sin, love the sinner* or *Pray the gay away.* Everything's going to be okay, you say?"

He walked toward me, his face filled with rage. "Excuse me if I tell you that you don't know a fucking thing about what it's going to be." He put his palms on my chest and shoved. Hard. "Get the hell away from me while you can before they start talking about you next. Go back to camp. Now." He shoved me again. I stumbled and fell on my butt.

"Don't tell me what to do, McGuire." I leaned forward.

"Jonathan, seriously, go back to camp now. Before you're missed." He knelt and looked me in the eyes. There was something besides anger written on his face. There was fear.

For me.

"I don't give a damn what people say."

We crouched there like two wrestlers waiting for the match to begin. Each of us tense, poised. Ready to attack. I reached for him first. I brushed my burned fingers across his cheek, damp from tears and smeared with ash from the fire.

It was all the permission he needed. He charged. His hands locked around my body, slamming me to the ground. He climbed on top of me.

"This is what you want?" He pinned my arms above my head and leaned down, his face inches from mine. He ground his hard-on against my leg. His breath, hot against my skin, ignited a fire in my body.

I nodded, unable to speak. He slid his hands under my T-shirt, pausing to pinch my nipples. I shuddered. My breath caught in my throat.

He yanked me into a sitting position. He sat on my lap, his legs wrapped around me in another wrestling move. I could feel my own erection pounding. Ian ripped his shirt off. Then he pulled my shirt over my head. The cool night air hit my skin.

He pushed me down on the ground again. The grass was soft, but the twigs dug into my skin. Birds chattered in the nearby trees as if they too were scandalized by what we were doing.

He climbed off me and stood up. Unzipped his pants and let them fall to his ankles. He towered, naked, above me. The scent of his body hit me.

"You're sure? This is what you want?" He stood, glowing in the moonlight.

He took my silence for consent.

Maybe it was.

He crawled on top of me again. His lips crushed mine in a fierce kiss. My hips lifted off the ground as I lost control and thrust at him. He moved his mouth to my ear. I groaned as he reached beneath me and grabbed my butt, pushing himself against my jeans.

I slid my arms around Ian's thin body. My hands touched the soft skin of his lower back where he curved toward me. He kissed me again, this time parting my lips with his tongue. I forgot how to breathe. His fingers fumbled with the button to my jeans.

"Wait!" I broke off our kiss. Pain shot through my hands as I grabbed his hands. "Please, just wait."

His breath came in short, hard gasps. His body shuddered against me. "Wait? Are you kidding me?"

Yes, my mind screamed.

No, my body disagreed.

One thought screamed in my mind: *I'm supposed to wait.*

"Wait?" he asked again.

For what?

I had no good answer to either question, his or mine.

He took my silence for consent.

Yeah, it was.

I released Ian's hands and closed my eyes. Felt the pressure of my jeans as Ian tugged on them. They got stuck, so I raised my hips to make it easier for him. The breeze hit me. I sucked in my breath from the shock of it.

And then the cool air disappeared, swallowed by a swirling hot, wet sea. I gasped.

He pulled away and smiled up at me, flecks of gold glinting in his eyes. A light wind blew through the forest and ran over my bare chest and arms and thighs. We were past the point of speaking. He ran his fingers down my side and hip. My muscles tightened. My chest heaved.

"Don't stop," I whispered and for once Ian obeyed. For one excruciating second, I balanced on the edge. Then I fell into the waves of heat and pressure that exploded until my veins ran hot. Panting, I lay on the ground at Porcupine Point and wondered what the hell I had done.

❖

Ian's body curled against mine, his head resting on my arm. Darkness pressed in on me as the urgent drive slipped away. I glanced at my body, naked and exposed for anyone to see. Drunk with shame, I lunged to my feet, stumbled and caught myself with my burned hands.

"Wait, Jonathan. Are you okay?" Ian reached for me.

Without thinking, I jerked away from his touch.

"Don't touch me!" I yanked my jeans up and pulled my T-shirt over my head.

Ian's eyes flooded with pain. Raw. Real.

I ran anyway.

At the edge of the clearing, I looked back for just a moment. Ian swayed and fell to the ground. He drew his legs to his bare chest and curled into himself. He shuddered, lifted his face, and our eyes connected. I watched his eyes narrow, his lips tighten, and the cold mask of anger harden on his face.

I turned and ran into the forest.

Jesus! I groped my way back to camp through the complete blackness of the forest. *Jesus! Jesus! Jesus!* The one word was all I could produce. It was a plea. It was a prayer. "Jesus, help me!" I lost my balance and lurched forward, disoriented, into the unknown.

CHAPTER TWENTY-ONE

Hey, Cooper, you awake?" Jake's ugly mug was the last thing I wanted to look at as I squinted into the bright morning light. Despite the events of the night before, the sun still rose on Thursday morning. The cabin still reeked of damp towels and dirty socks. Bryan still sat in his bunk, frying mosquitos with the bloodlust of a death-row executioner. Outside the chickadees still chattered, and in the distance Edward and Bella still called to each other.

Jake leaned against the ladder on the bunk bed we still had to share for two more days and glanced at Aaron's empty cot.

"Go to hell." I climbed out of bed and faced him.

"Jeez, Coop. What crawled up your ass and died? You used to have a sense of humor." Jake looked around the cluttered cabin at the other campers who were digging through their duffel bags, ignoring us.

"This is the one and only time I'm going to say this, Jake, so you'd better pay close attention because there won't be a remedial class, like you're used to. If I hear one word about you harassing Ian again, just one word, you'll answer to me. Understand?"

"Is that supposed to be a threat?" Jake laughed. "You may have everyone else here fooled, but I've always known what you were. You don't deserve her."

"What the hell are you talking about? Who don't I deserve?"

"*Jonathan* this and *Jonathan* that. You're all she talks about until I'm ready to puke." His voice cracked and a lot of things became clear to me. Jake hadn't been gunning for Ian at all. He had been aiming for me, and Ian had just been caught in the crossfire.

I pushed past Jake and walked out of the cabin, slamming the screen door as I left. The morning was already hot and muggy. A string of profanity ran through my mind. There weren't enough curse words in my vocabulary to describe what I wished would happen to Jake. My feet pounded along the path to the boys' shower, kicking up dust as I went. *What if Ian's in there?* I panicked. An image of him, naked, flashed into my mind. My stomach cramped and my head felt light. *Oh God, I ran. I left him all alone.*

I stomped down the narrow forest trail. *Warriors,* I thought, *don't freak out. They don't run and leave a man behind.* My feet pounded the rhythm over and over on the ground as I thought of all the other things warriors don't do that I had done.

That we had done together.

Simon was up early, painting down by the shore of Spirit Lake. I closed my eyes and immersed myself in the memory of the world beneath the lake's surface where Ian's crushing strength had once turned gentle. My hands clenched. Pain shot through my burned fingers, and I cringed.

❖

I scanned the dining hall and breathed a sigh of relief. Ian was nowhere in sight. Odd glances followed me as I made my way to Curtain Call's usual table where MacKenzie and Kari sat with Sara, too absorbed in their conversation to even look at me.

"Morning, Jonathan." The smile on Sara's face didn't quite make it to her eyes. Ian walked in the dining room. He arrived the way previews do at a movie. Everyone hushed and fixed their attention on him. Cheeks burning bright red, head held high, he made his way through the breakfast line. He took my breath away.

Ian looked at me as he walked past us. My body burned in every place he had touched me the night before. I searched his face for some sign of connection or recognition. Nothing.

"Hey, Ian, join us for breakfast?" I called out to him. He turned his head and walked away, not even bothering to answer me.

"Wait, Ian!" I started to move toward him, but Sara's hand on my arm stopped me.

"No," she said. I looked at her and, for one crazy moment, considered confiding in her. Everything about her—her lip piercing, her crazy hair, her glitter eyeliner—said cool. Except her eyes. They said, *Let him go.*

I rushed past her, past the questioning eyes, out the dining hall, past Simon who waved and smiled, past the willow tree that couldn't possibly shield me from this, down Warrior's Way, and entered the guys' shower room.

I didn't know the two guys who were showering, but they sure knew me. One guy grabbed a towel and bolted out of the shower. The other guy turned his back to me to finish rinsing his hair, and then he left the shower room too.

"Fucking fags." He slammed his locker. The door banged shut, and I shook with relief. Alone in the shower room, I cranked the hot water knob and stood beneath the scalding water until my skin throbbed.

He hates me. He hates me. Oh God, he hates me. My head spun. *And I don't blame him.*

I leaned against the wall and breathed in the thick, hot air. Let him go? Impossible. But what else could I do? Stand with him in the open for everyone to see? Equally impossible.

I toweled off, filled the porcelain sink, and plunged my burned hands into the cool water. In a flash the room erupted in blinding light and spun. Sparkles danced in my eyes. In and out, in and out, I panted until my breathing steadied and the pain subsided. I searched my reflection in the rippling metal mirror.

You're that guy, aren't you? I asked the stranger in the mirror. *The guy who unsettles everyone.*

Don't Ask, Don't Tell suddenly made a lot of sense.

Chapter Twenty-two

Ian didn't show up for Curtain Call practice. Sara pitched a fit, and I almost reminded her that she had stopped me from going after him, but I didn't. Besides, I was sure I'd see him at lunch and we'd sit together like we always did and I would tell him I was sorry and he would understand and it would be okay. But he didn't show up at lunch, and I wound up eating burritos and beans with Bryan. When Ian was also a no-show at sculpture, I wheedled it out of Simon that Ian was claiming to be sick and that Hannah had brought lunch to him in his cabin. She must have brought him dinner too because he didn't show up for that either.

By Friday morning I was pretty sure the last day of camp, the last golden day of freedom, would be spent without so much as a glimpse of Ian.

Paul had announced an end-of-camp gathering at the lake, and I sat on the beach, the gritty sand burning my legs as Dawn played her spirit drum. It was a beautiful instrument, Ojibwe in origin, with eagle feathers that fluttered in the wind. Her hands stroked the drum and the drum responded, producing a haunting sound that moved through me. It would have been a perfect moment, except Ian wasn't there to share it with me. I looked for him and was surprised to spot him sitting away from the rest of us, his face as dead and taut as the elk hide on Dawn's drumhead.

Paul walked down to the beach carrying a stool, a bar of soap, and a towel. He stepped into the still lake and placed the three-legged stool in the water.

"As our time together comes to an end, I thought we would speak today about how to follow Christ. I know of no better way to illustrate this than to follow His example. I ask each of you to remove your shoes, come forward, and sit on the stool in front of me."

Sara slipped off her sandals, walked forward, and took a seat on the stool. Paul surprised everyone by kneeling in the water, lifting each of Sara's feet, and lathering them with soap. Then he rinsed her feet in the lake and dried them with the towel.

"Please, each of you, come forward."

One by one the other counselors and campers made their way to Paul, who washed everyone's feet. I couldn't. Not after what I'd done. What we'd done. Except it wasn't about what we'd done together. It was about what I had done to him. Running out on him. Leaving him to face this all alone. Tears threatened to spill down my face. The wind stirred and the long branches of the willow swayed in the breeze.

"Come, Jonathan," Paul called to me. I stood, slipped off my flip-flops, walked to the edge of the lake, and sat on the stool. Paul lathered my feet with soap, touching places of pain I hadn't even known existed. When he finished, he dipped them back into the lake. I couldn't hold back the tears as I made my way back to my seat. Ian was nowhere to be seen; he had not accepted Paul's invitation.

My breath caught in my throat when Simon pushed his wheelchair right to the edge of Spirit Lake. Paul reached forward and lifted Simon's lifeless limbs, one at a time, folding up the footplates. He untied Simon's shoes, removed his socks, and rolled his pants legs up, exposing his atrophied calves and limp feet. Simon's smile held no hint of shame. Paul lowered each of Simon's feet into the water. I knew he couldn't feel the water. I knew he could only see Paul's hands moving in the ritualistic washing of his feet, but based on the emotions that played across Simon's face, I also knew he felt as much if not more than anyone else who had received Paul's blessing.

"Thank you, my brother, for blessing me today." Paul placed Simon's feet back on the footplates of his wheelchair, pushed him out of the lake, and turned to address us. "I want you to imagine that you are not sitting on the beach at Spirit Lake. Picture yourselves living in the dusty desert, walking in hot and dirty sand every day, using your feet to spur on your smelly camel. I want you to imagine a time before indoor plumbing and daily showers. Now, I want you to imagine that you've arrived at someone's home as a guest after a long and exhausting journey. Would there be any greater joy than being welcomed into your friend's house where a servant rushed to submerse your burning hot feet in cool water, washing away the grime of your long journey?" Paul cupped his hands and scooped up water, letting it run between his fingers. "Now, imagine that today it was not I, it was not even the lowest servant in a home who washed your feet. Imagine it was your Savior, Jesus Christ. When I look out at all of your faces, I see such cause for Christ to rejoice! You are powerful lights of truth in a fallen world. Tomorrow morning, your parents will arrive for parents' day, and I want each of you to remember how precious you are in God's eyes as you go in peace and serve the Lord."

❖

"Jonathan, I'd like to speak with you." Paul stopped me as I walked toward the dining hall for lunch. "Do you have a moment?"

He knows. Fear shot through me like a bolt of electricity. My teeth throbbed, and my mouth tasted like metal. I followed him into his office.

"Have a seat." Paul waved toward the chair across from his desk.

I sat and faced him, my stomach rolling like Spirit Lake on a stormy day. "A few campers came to see me this morning. They had a concern they thought I should know about. Evidently, something happened at the bonfire the other night, but I want to hear your thoughts about it."

"Someone stole Ian's notebook and read from it in front of everyone."

"I understand that someone was Jake."

"Yeah. He threw it in the fire." I couldn't keep the anger out of my voice. I looked at the stuffed deer head mounted on the wall above Paul's desk, the tackle box and fishing pole that leaned in the corner, the gleaming rifles locked in the cabinet. The scent of dead fish and gun oil hung in the air. I thought about Jake stealing Ian's journal and reading his most private thoughts for anyone to hear. I wanted to shout. I wanted to scream. Instead I stared at the white curtain that blew in the wind and listened to the songbirds' chatter through the open window. Probably trying to agree on their travel plans for heading south soon.

"I was told that you followed Ian into the woods. That you didn't get back to your cabin until late in the night, and when you did, you were upset. Is that true?"

I had thought everyone was asleep. I had thought wrong.

"Jonathan, I'm concerned about your relationship with Ian." Paul paused, struggling with the decision to say more. "I have been praying about whether or not I should talk with you about my worries, but this morning, I realized that I have a responsibility to reach out to you. You've grown up here, and I care about you as if you were my son."

He placed his hand on my arm, avoiding my burned hands. Sweat broke out along my forehead, and I struggled to take a deep breath.

"I think it's possible that you are under some kind of satanic attack right now, and you are being tempted by the flesh to deviate from your true identity in Christ. I know you have been raised to know God and to obey His Word, so I know you are aware of the Bible's warnings against the kind of feelings that I suspect you are having for Ian. I'd like to pray with you, Jonathan. I'd like to ask God to protect you from having this sin of the flesh take root in your spirit. Would you please pray with me?"

A breeze blew through the window and stirred the ash from his pipe that lay on his desk. The air filled with the pungent smell of stale tobacco.

I couldn't look at Paul, much less give him an answer, so I hung my head. It looked like I was praying, but inside, I was dying.

"Father God, we come before You today with such a painful situation." Paul's voice thundered through me. "Jonathan has lost his way, Lord. He has been lured by the enemy to indulge sinful thoughts and urges. Lord, You know the full truth of all that has transpired."

My stomach heaved at that thought.

Paul continued, "I ask that You intervene in Jonathan's and Ian's lives. I ask that You surround them with a hedge of protection so that the enemy cannot penetrate their pure hearts and thoughts. Lord, I pray that You will help them break this bondage to sin and reclaim their true identities as sons and heirs to the kingdom of heaven. In Your name, I pray, amen."

He raised his head and smiled at me. Tears were in his eyes and love, yes, love shone at me, but it didn't make the vomit that had collected in my mouth taste any better.

Satanic attack? Bondage to sin? I stumbled to my feet and backed toward the door. The vomit burned the back of my throat, and no amount of swallowing or praying could keep it down.

"I'm sorry." I didn't look back. He called out something about getting my hands looked at, but the venom crept through me, inching toward my core. I ran through the hallways of the oppressively hot administration building. There was no time to have my hands examined by the camp nurse. There was barely enough time to reach the back side of the kitchen where I bent over and puked into a garbage container that reeked of decaying meat.

What if Paul is right? The thought doubled me over again as another wave of nausea hit.

CHAPTER TWENTY-THREE

I walked away from the garbage with my emotions and my stomach still heaving. Past the outdoor theater and toward the beach. Down the dock where I sat, feet dangling into the lake.

Lord—I sent my prayer adrift like a message in a bottle—*are You there? Do You still hear my voice?* "Why is loving him so wrong?"

"Who said it is?" In my intense concentration I had not heard the thumping sound of Simon's wheelchair approaching. He read the pain written all over my face. "I had a feeling we weren't done talking the other day. Are you okay?" Simon locked his wheelchair and looked at me.

I dropped my head, unable to meet his eyes. The whitened eyes of a belly-up floater fish stared at me through the worn wooden slats in the dock. The stench of rot and foam and seaweed wafted up from the lake.

"No, I don't think I am."

"Want to talk about it?"

"You wouldn't understand."

"What it feels like to be different? What it feels like to be talked about? Stared at? Try me."

He had a point. "Jake did something that hurt Ian, and I felt so bad for him. He ran off into the woods. I couldn't let him be out there in the darkness alone, so I followed him. I found him crying so I held him. Suddenly we were touching and I didn't stop it… didn't *want* to stop it, God help me. Simon, I think about that, and I feel all these things that I'm supposed to feel for a girl, but I don't. I never did. What's wrong with me?" The water gurgled under the dock and I wondered how long it takes for a dead fish to finally sink and go away.

"First, let me tell you that you are safe. It's okay to talk about these things with me. Second, I want you to hear this loud and clear: there is nothing wrong with you, Jonathan. You just have feelings waking up inside of you that are in conflict with what you've been taught to believe."

"After Ian and I…well…I had to get out of there. I ran. I left him alone." The sun beat down on me through the heavy, humid air, and I felt the first bite of a burn spread over my face and arms and legs. "He hates me."

"And you love him?"

"I don't know. I don't know anything anymore."

"So let's try to make some sense of this, okay? Let's start by getting real with each other. What do you feel for Ian?"

"It…it hurts."

"Why?"

"Because whenever I look at him, I don't know who I am."

"Okay, what else?"

"I get this rush of emotions and…other feelings when I'm around him." Heat spread over my face.

"You're talking about being physically attracted to him."

"Guys talk all the time about how hot this girl or that girl is, and I never felt that way before, but when I'm with Ian, I get it. It's more than just the physical stuff, though. I care about him. I could have killed Jake when he hurt Ian. Then I hurt him even worse." I pictured Ian, curled up and in pain in the woods. The tears I had been fighting spilled down my face.

"It's going to be okay."

"How can it be? God says this is wrong." My face flushed with sweat. I felt feverish. "God says who I am is wrong."

"Do you think God ever created someone He thought was a mistake?"

"No," I blurted out.

"That's right. You are His beloved child. Who you are is not a mistake because God doesn't make mistakes."

"Paul knows, Simon. He says I'm in bondage to sin. And my parents? Do you know what they would say?" A stale, hot wind blew off the lake and pressed down on me.

Simon's face darkened with anger. "I said God doesn't make mistakes. I didn't say anything about *people* not making mistakes. Believe me, people are capable of making terrible mistakes."

"Simon, I need to know if feeling this, being like this…" I struggled to put into words the dread that had been growing in me.

"If being a gay man puts you outside of God's grace. That's what you want to know, right?" Simon finished my sentence.

The words *gay man* thundered in my ears. I cringed and nodded.

"Have you read the Old Testament?"

"Enough to know that it frowns on being gay, to put it mildly."

"True. Have you read the *whole* Old Testament?"

"No, I guess not. I always meant to."

"It always amazes me how few Christians have actually read the whole Bible, especially the Old Testament. Did you know that the Old Testament also states that if there is mold in your bathroom you need to have a priest come into your home and examine it?"

"No way!" The words erupted out of my mouth. "Where does it say that?"

"Read Leviticus. You'll find that there are lots of things in the Old Testament that most Christians don't follow. For example, there's a lot of stuff in there about polygamy and slavery being okay. Did you know that?" In the distance a huge flock of birds rose up out of the forest and scattered in different directions, cawing their warnings to each other.

"Yeah, actually I did. I just never thought about it before." My mind spun at Simon's words. "How come you know all this stuff?"

"You remember I told you about when I was in the hospital after my accident? Even though I was angry with God at that time, I still clung to my beliefs like a lifeline. One of those beliefs was that gay people were choosing a lifestyle that led them away from God. Of course, I had never known an openly gay person before. Then I was assigned a physical therapist named Sam. He was the most patient person I'd ever met. Every ounce of the physical strength and a great deal of the emotional strength that I have today, I owe to Sam. He pushed me when I needed to be pushed and he listened when I needed to yell. One day Sam's boyfriend, Patrick, picked him up at work. They were going out for dinner to celebrate their twelfth anniversary. I remember thinking—*twelfth* anniversary? Weren't gay guys just about casual relationships that were based on sex? But Sam and Patrick clearly loved each other. It got me thinking about why God would have a problem with two people loving each other. I had a lot of time on my hands, and I was already in a place where I was drilling God with some hard questions, so I threw that one in there too, and after a lot of praying and reading the Bible, I came up with one question that I just couldn't get over."

"What was that?"

"When did it become okay for the people who hold the Bible to be God's absolute truth to choose which parts of it to enforce, like the sections about homosexuality, and which parts to write off as not applying to us anymore, like the parts about slavery or polygamy?"

"I always thought that we had to take the Bible as God's word. You know, literally. All of it."

"I did too, Jonathan, but the problem is that the meaning of words changes throughout the years. Take the word homosexuality, for example. Did you know that it never actually appears in the Bible? However, when the Bible was written it was quite common for a man to sodomize another man after defeating him in a battle. Some places, like Sodom, treated newcomers to their city that way. It was rape, not love—and yes, the God I know would absolutely disapprove of such brutality, then and today. He would call that an abomination. But two people, in love and committed to one another? No, Jonathan, I don't see God calling that an abomination. Did you ever read 1 and 2 Samuel?"

"Yeah, I read all about Jonathan and David."

"What did you think about their story?"

"I think they loved each other." Thousands of brilliant lights danced off the whitecaps on the lake and hurt my eyes. I had to squint to take it all in.

"So do I, and many Biblical scholars agree with us. They believe that King David, a man after God's own heart, and Jonathan shared a love that we would describe today as a committed, loving homosexual relationship."

"I thought maybe I was just seeing something I wanted to see. I guess I thought it wasn't possible to be gay and a man after God's heart. That's what has been tearing me apart."

"For now I'm going to give you a different question to try to answer: What does God want most from you?"

"I don't know. I'm not sure."

"Think about it. I believe you'll find when you can answer that question, you will see a lot of things more clearly. Now tell me this, what are you the most afraid of?"

"That if I am myself, really myself, God, my family, and my friends won't love me anymore."

"Because you're gay."

"Yeah, because I'm gay." I said the words aloud for the first time. The truth of the statement shook me.

"In my experience, loving isn't a choice. It's a state of being."

One of the loons called out from across the lake, breaking the stillness of the moment.

"Tell that to Ian's parents."

"Yes, I know about that. I like to think that on some level, they still love him, but they just can't stand by him through this. I don't see what good that kind of love does a person, and I'm not going to pretend that I can understand them. Instead I'm going to ask you: If God's love actually is unconditional, even if the people closest to you fail you, would it be enough?"

"I'll think about it, okay?"

"Sure. I'll look forward to hearing your thoughts when you've chewed on it a bit. There's one other thing, though, that I would be remiss if I didn't say. Being physically intimate with someone is a powerful thing. It is something that should only be entered into when you are ready. Understand?"

"Thanks, Simon. I don't know what I would do if I couldn't talk to you about this."

"Anytime, my friend, and I mean that. Now isn't there someone else you need to talk to?"

I groaned. "Do I have to?"

"No, you could sit here, yakking at me all day until we turn into fish-flavored Krispy Kremes." Simon grinned. "Or you could go face the music. Own up to Ian and ask for forgiveness."

"And if he won't forgive me?"

"You'll still feel better knowing that you tried to make amends."

❖

I hurried along the lower trail of Spirit Lake.

"*Boozhoo, Needjee.*" Dawn and Bear emerged from a connecting trail. "You missed the nature hike." She stated it as a fact, without judgment. A stench rose off Bear who hung his tail and ears in misery.

"Was it today? I'm sorry, I meant to go." I stepped away from Bear and put my hand to my nose. "Whew, Bear, you're ripe. What did you get into, fella?"

"This stupid dog thinks he is a spaniel, evidently. He flushed out a skunk and, as you can smell, the skunk won. *Makwa* has no common sense." Dawn grinned. I suspected she enjoyed Bear's naughtiness as much as the rest of us did.

"I don't know, maybe he took the skunk spray so no one else would have to." I looked at Bear's rich brown eyes, the color of melted chocolate.

"You have such a good heart. You always see the good in things. But *you* don't have to give *Makwa* a tomato-juice bath!" Bear's head swiveled up to look at Dawn. He let out a low whimper. "Don't worry about missing the nature hike. You have had other things on your mind."

"Yeah, I have."

"It happens." Dawn's ability to speak truth in two words never failed to impress me. Acceptance came so easily to her. "You are on your own walk now, *Needjee*."

"I guess I am." Light broke through the forest roof and highlighted a leaf, then a twig, revealing startling bursts of color in a world that could be mistaken as dark and dreary. "See you later, Dawn."

"*Ayaangwaamizin*—sorry, be careful. This dog has me thinking in Ojibwe again. Seriously though, I don't like what I'm hearing in the wind. Keep an eye on the sky today."

"Okay, will do." I left Dawn and Bear—who seemed to have understood the word *bath* and looked worried—and followed the trail that led to Porcupine Point. In the distance Bear howled his protest. *You brought this on yourself, buddy.* The thought made me uneasy.

"Hey." I stepped into the clearing. "I was hoping you'd be here."

"What the hell do you want?" Ian stood at the precipice of the cliff. His eyes shone brighter than normal as if he had just finished crying. *Oh my God, he's even more beautiful than I remembered.* I couldn't breathe.

"Ian, I'm sorry." I crossed the clearing to where he stood, "I'm so sorry. After we, you know. Well, I freaked."

"Yeah, that's a fair summation." He squared off, arms crossed, and stared me down.

"So, you understand?"

"Hell no, I don't understand. You ran. Two nights ago you left me here after what we shared, and you ran. I don't need to listen to any more of your bullshit." Ian began to walk away.

"Wait, I need to tell you something."

He whipped around. "You *need*? What do I give a shit about what you need?"

Heat rose up from the ground and pushed down on me from the sky above me. It reached out from the forest and up from the lake that had begun to churn and kick up a spray.

"Did you give a shit about what I needed when I lay here, the taste of you still in my mouth, and you ran because you couldn't handle it? And now you need to talk to me about something?"

Guilty. On all counts.

The blue sky disappeared as a wall of clouds rolled in from the north.

"Yeah, I do."

"Too bad I don't feel the burning need to listen." Ian pushed past me. "Not anymore."

He couldn't leave, not like this. I spun him around. My hands clamped on his triceps, and I pressed my lips against the hard ridges of his scowl, half expecting him to soften and yield to me and I took the punch full in the gut.

"Leave me the hell alone, Jonathan." He said my name the way he said *fuck you*. I hit the ground gasping as he disappeared into the bush that led to the forest.

"Wait, Ian. Stay with me." But it was too late. He was already gone.

Chapter Twenty-four

"Why?" I yelled after Ian. "Why can't you understand this? You see everything else about me, but you don't get that these feelings scare the crap out of me." I crouched on all fours on the hard dirt ground at the precipice of Porcupine Point. Sucking wind. Trying to catch my breath long after my gut had recovered from Ian's punch. The air felt different. Heavier and thicker. The temperature dropped and the wind blew off the lake with the attitude of someone ready to pick a fight. The golden glow from the sun disappeared behind a thick veil of low-hanging clouds that churned in a way that made me nervous. Cold, clammy chills ran over my flesh. I was alone, staring at the small opening in the bush, willing him to come back.

He didn't.

Each second that passed confirmed what I already knew. Whatever had existed between us was dead. I had murdered it.

He can't understand this because he doesn't know Me as you do. The answer pushed itself into my mind.

"That's no excuse. He knows me." I spat my anger out at God and immediately tasted the lie.

In the distance the emergency horn blasted. All campers were to return to the safety of the main lodge. I pictured Paul searching the sky for signs of danger, leaning toward the radio, listening. The wind swept up the cliff and almost knocked me over. A low, rippling cloud ceiling rolled in, backlit and underbrushed like a charcoal sketch. I ducked through the small opening in the bush that led to the forest.

My watch glowed 5:15 p.m., but the forest was oddly dark. I walked along the upper trail with my hands in front of me, groping for tree trunks to guide me. A bolt of lightning shattered the sky, lighting up the white birch trees. The only sounds in the forest were the wailing of the wind and the thundering beat of my heart. My eyes darted for signs that I was still on the right trail. Ian's voice taunted me. *You sing it and dance it and walk it and talk it. You hallelujah and amen in all the right spots.* I stumbled over a root, toppled forward, and grabbed for a tree to catch myself with burned hands.

Yup, that's me. I winced. At least it was before I met Ian. I tried to swallow the blame I wanted to place on him, but my gut rebelled. A rush of acid filled my mouth and tasted of more lies. I stumbled on the offshoot to the lower trail and slid down the muddy decline to the trail that led back to camp and Paul.

Under attack of the enemy...in bondage to sin...the man of the family now. Thunder crashed in the dark sky. Lightning flashed, scary close. The trees thinned and provided less shelter as I neared the camp. The heavy, thick air that had been crushing me relaxed. Fat drops of rain coated my arms and face, and I searched the sky that churned a sickening shade of green into the charcoal clouds, but there were no answers there either.

The muscles of my chest cramped. I sucked the cold air in between my clenched teeth and blew it out. Short and hard and angry. Raindrops multiplied like broken promises and hurled their accusations on my head.

"Please forgive me!" The howling wind drowned out my voice. The strong branches of the fir trees swayed wildly. A fierce breeze swept off Spirit Lake and rattled through the trees. Even the leaves fluttered their judgment of me as I pulled my thin shirt tighter against my body and leaned into the wind.

I stepped out of the forest and into a world I didn't recognize. The heavy split-pea sky hung low, bathing the camp in an eerie green light. Wind screamed, shrill and high pitched. The emergency horn blasted. Adrenaline pulsed through my body and my hands flew to my ears, but did little good. The strong trees thrashed in the wind. The young ones, not much more than twigs, snapped in two. Willow, my willow, tossed to a frenzied beat. The dark gray surface of the lake crashed in protest. The air tasted of dirt and exposed marrow from the twisted and downed trees that scattered the campground. Tucking my head, I ran against the wind and the rain, weaving and ducking to dodge the debris. A shutter flew past me. Shingles pelted me. The screen door to the boathouse wrenched off its hinges and flew through the air, just missing me. Even the camp buildings were out to get me.

I blew into the lodge like a scandal. Rain and mud splattered anyone close to me. Simon, Dawn, and most of the Curtain Call cast were huddled by the crackling fire that filled the room with light and warmth. The smoke of burning applewood mixed with the spicy scent of Hannah's chili and fresh-baked corn bread.

"Jonathan, oh thank God." Simon broke speed limits as he wheeled over to me. "We've been so worried about you and Ian." He looked behind me.

"Ian?" Simon's words hit me like a second punch. Tremors ran across my body. "You mean he's not here?"

"He's not with you?"

"No. He isn't. I thought he'd be here." I scanned the lodge: people sat at the tables, stood by the fire, watched the storm from the windows as if it were a freaking reality TV show. Someone cranked the radio's volume to unbearable. An obnoxious triple beep blasted through the lodge and silenced everyone. A newscaster began speaking:

The National Weather Service in Cook County has detected a severe thunderstorm capable of producing golf-ball-sized hail and damaging winds in excess of sixty miles per hour. This storm is located near Grand Marais, moving east at thirty miles per hour. This is a dangerous storm. People outside should move to a shelter, inside a strong building and away from windows. Large hail, damaging winds, and continuous cloud-to-ground lightning is occurring with this storm. Move indoors immediately. Remember: if you can hear thunder, you are close enough to be struck by lightning. This warning is in effect until one thirty a.m.

An explosion of chatter erupted in the lodge. Hannah rushed out of the kitchen with a large towel and wrapped it around my drenched body. "Go sit by the fire, honey, you're freezing."

"I can't, Hannah. He's missing." I shrugged the towel off and put my hand on the door handle.

"Wait, what are you doing?" Simon's eyes flew open with concern.

"I've got to go find him. I can't leave him out there. Not again." My voice rose to a wail on par with the wind. Heads turned, but I ignored them. Simon wheeled in front of me, blocking the door.

"Now think this through. Do you have any idea where he might be?"

"In the forest. Maybe along the upper trail."

Dawn looked up from where she sat at the fireplace and spoke, "The spot where you were praying that night? I know where it is. I'll go." She stood, put on her raincoat, and grabbed a flashlight and a walkie-talkie. Bear howled in protest. She leaned down to the whining dog and whispered, "It's all right. It's just a lot of light and noise. *Gego zegiziken, Makwa.* There's nothing to fear. Bethany, would you watch him for me?" Dawn held Bear's leash toward her. "You're going to have to hold his leash tight, or he'll bolt out into the storm after me."

"I will." Bethany took the leash from Dawn and turned to me. She looked scared. "You're not actually going out in this, are you, Jonathan?"

"Of course he's not." Paul strode from the window where he had been looking at the sky. Everything about him said his decision was final. I felt myself bending beneath his will. Images of Ian with hands curled into fists flashed through my mind. His spirit, his strength, and probably a big chunk of his stupidity seeped into me.

I pictured my father, holding the Medal of Honor he'd earned on his first tour of duty for going back for the body of a fallen soldier only to discover the soldier was still alive. *I just did what any good soldier doe*s, he'd told me. *Leave no man behind, that's the Marine way.*

"Yes, I am." I grabbed a raincoat and put it on. Took another for when I found Ian. I couldn't even think the word *if.* Dawn handed me the second walkie-talkie.

"Jonathan, Dawn, I forbid this. It's dangerous. You will both stay here inside this lodge where you are safe." Paul spoke with his best sermon-giving voice. It boomed through the room.

"And what about Ian?" I spun around to face him. "Or don't you care about him, Paul?"

"I will not put the life of a person at this camp at risk by allowing you or Dawn to go out into this storm. It's right on top of us! We will wait until it subsides, and then I'll go out to find him."

Simon turned his wheelchair to face Paul. "You *are* putting the life of a person at this camp at risk. You are risking Ian's life, and the best chance that boy has of surviving this storm is standing in front of you. Jonathan was the last person with Ian. He knows where he should begin looking, and Dawn knows that forest better than anyone I know." Simon's eyes strayed to Dawn. Something unspoken passed between them. "We have to trust God, Paul. He will guide Jonathan to Ian."

An unmistakable look of repulsion crossed Paul's face. Just for a second, but I saw it.

"I'm going, Paul. With or without your blessing." No one spoke to Paul like that, but I didn't give a damn. I finally understood what was wrong with Don't Ask, Don't Tell.

Paul walked away without another word. Dawn and I pushed open the lodge door, unleashing the rain that fell on us like a stoning and splattered Simon. His face, filled with concern, flashed into view for a brief moment before the door slammed shut. Dawn and I leaned into the straight-line wind that raged off the lake, slamming against the camp and anyone foolish enough to brave it. Dawn grabbed my arm and together we charged back into hell.

As if the sheets of pounding rain and wind weren't enough, the sky opened up and hurled Ping-Pong ball sized hail at us. We sprinted across the campground and ducked into the forest where the biggest issues were slippery trails and darkness. If I hadn't known better, I would have guessed it was the middle of the night.

"What do you think? Stay together or split up?" Dawn asked me once she'd caught her breath.

"I think we should split up. We can cover more distance that way. Find him faster." It surprised me how easily I assumed command. It surprised me even more how easily Dawn followed my lead.

"Okay, but keep in touch on the walkie-talkie. Take the high trail where you saw him last. I'll follow the lower trail in case he got lost and wandered off," Dawn shouted into the wind.

"Sounds good. Thanks for coming with me. It means a lot."

"You're doing the right thing. Now ask God to guide you to Ian. He'll help you find him."

I clicked on my flashlight and began the slick climb up the steep incline to the upper trail. I stumbled and slid back down. My knees bashed against the protruding rocks. Determined, I grabbed the rocks and scaled the incline like a rock climber until I reached the familiar upper trail and stood outside the bush that led to Porcupine Point.

"Ian, are you in there?" The screaming wind was my only answer. "Ian, where are you?" It howled in my ears. An owl screeched, ahead of me and farther down the upper trail. I followed its call. When the trail dead-ended, I turned and pushed through the thick bushes into uncharted territory. My foot landed wrong on a root and my ankle twisted. Jolts of pain shot through my foot and into my leg. Hot tears sprang to my eyes, and I bit my lip to stop from yelling out, took a tentative step, screamed, and crashed to the ground in excruciating pain.

The darkness closed in on me, the same way it had when Ian punched me. "Help me!" I sobbed to God, to my father, maybe to both of them. Was it rain or my own tears that fell from my chin? There was no way to be certain. My panting breath slowed. The tingling began in my hands and moved to my arms, down my chest, and into my legs until all my empty places filled with warmth. I stood and limped forward, pushing my way through a thicket of bushes that scratched my hands and wrists, leaving long red claw marks on my exposed skin. I stepped into a small clearing that was being pummeled by rain. A pile of dirty rags lay in the center of the clearing.

"Ian, where are you?"

"Jonathan? Is that you?" The pile of rags rose up from the dip in the ground. Filthy and plastered with dirt and leaves, he looked at me through calm eyes. I hopped and fell on the ground next to him. We clung to each other as wind and rain and hail pounded disapproval on our heads.

"Yeah, it's me. We've got to get back to the lodge." I wrapped the raincoat around his thin, shivering shoulders.

"What the hell do you think you're doing out in this?" Ian's voice outshouted the thunder.

I ignored him and reached for my walkie-talkie. "Dawn, I found him. We're heading back to the lodge." I struggled to stand up and fell back to the ground.

"Scratch that, Dawn," Ian shouted into the walkie-talkie. "Jonathan hurt his ankle. There's no way we can make it all the way to the lodge."

Dawn's voice crackled through the yellow walkie-talkie in Ian's hand. "Can you get to my cabin?"

"Yeah, I think so."

"There's a first-aid kit in the bathroom. Wrap his ankle with an elastic bandage and apply ice. Make a fire to get warm and eat something. I'm going to wait it out in one of the girls' cabins until this blows over. I'll come as soon as I can and check on you. Call Paul from my cabin. Let him know where we are and that we're safe."

"Okay."

"Ian, it's good to hear your voice." Dawn signed off.

"You're going to have to lean on me." Ian knelt and I wrapped my arm around his shoulders. He tried to pull me into a standing position, but pain shot up my entire leg. I collapsed on the ground, panting.

"Are you freaking kidding me? Get it together. Get off your ass and come with me *now*." The tone of his voice snapped me to attention. *That's the Ian I know and—*

I leaned my full weight on him and surrendered to his strength.

Chapter Twenty-five

Dawn's cabin was unlocked. Outside the wind screamed and the sky burst open with lightning and thunder aimed right at us.

"Come here," he ordered. "I want to take a look at your ankle."

I sat down on the cold fireplace hearth and held my ankle out to him. Ian knelt and rolled my pants cuff up.

"Oh man, that looks bad." He shook his head.

I looked down and saw my ankle, already swollen and turning purple. He stomped into the bathroom and returned with dry towels and the first-aid kit. Ian threw the towel at me and bent to concentrate on stabilizing my ankle with an elastic bandage. When he had finished wrapping my foot, he went into the kitchen and returned with a bag of ice. I jumped as the cold and weight of the bag hit my ankle.

"Quit being such a baby," he snapped. "Jeez, Jonathan, what were you thinking?"

"There was no way I was leaving you stranded in the forest again."

He looked at me, and his eyes softened for a moment before the cold glare returned. "Paul blew the emergency horn. You should have gone to the lodge where it was safe. Coming to look for me was stupid." Ian attacked a stack of newspaper by the fireplace, crumpling sheets and hurling them into the fireplace. "How many times do I have to tell you that I don't need you to come to my rescue? I can handle myself."

Stupid! Me and my stupid erroneous assumptions. "I'm sorry. I know you can. You were doing exactly what you were supposed to do. Lying low until the storm passed. Not like me, stumbling around like an idiot and spraining my ankle. At least I hope it's just a sprain."

"Can you move your toes?" He threw small branches on top of the newspaper and refused to look at my foot. It hurt, but I wiggled my heart out. He lit a match and held it to the newspaper.

"I think it's just a sprain."

"See? You'll be running out on people again before you know it." The flames devoured the paper and licked at the white bark on the small birch branches. Black smoke billowed out at us.

"I'm sorry, Ian. I really am."

"It's going to hurt like hell, but you're going to be fine." The fire crackled as the logs were consumed in flame. Thick smoke swirled around us. Ian reached forward and opened the flue.

"I'm sorry," I said again.

"You're absolutely, one hundred percent right. You are sorry, and I'm sick of apologies. They don't change anything." He fumed and walked to Dawn's desk. He picked up her landline and pressed the button marked *Lodge*. "Hey, Paul…Yeah, Jonathan found me. We made it to Dawn's cabin. She's holed up in one of the girls' cabins. We're safe, but Jonathan is going to need some crutches… Yeah, he sprained his ankle." The windowpanes rattled from the force of the wind that pummeled the small cabin. The door jumped in its frame. Lightning flashed, followed by a deafening crash of thunder. "No, we are not going to try for the lodge. Not yet. We'll stay here until this blows over—Paul? Are you there? Paul? Phone's dead." He slammed the phone on the charger, stared out the window, and suppressed a shiver.

"Hey, Ian, it's warmer over here." He turned around, looked at me. He shivered again and looked at the crackling fire. My thoughts wandered to the night of the bonfire when more than my hands had burned.

"You're blushing. Why?"

Was that a hint of softness in his voice I heard? My heart thudded in my chest.

"I don't know." Less than five feet separated us in Dawn's small living room. It might as well have been five thousand miles.

"Yes, you do."

The wind howled and battered the small cabin. I could see the trees whipping through the rain-streaked window.

"Ian, I…I—"

"*A…N*. Yup, that's my name. Good, now can you form any other words? Should we try Jonathan now?" A slight smile played on his lips.

"Ian, I don't know how to do this." There, I'd said it.

"Clearly."

"Do you? Is this so simple for you that you never struggle with it?"

"No, it isn't. Nothing about this is simple, but at least I'm not pretending to be someone I'm not."

"You're right. I have been hiding from everyone. Paul, my parents, my friends. But don't you understand? I couldn't let them see the real me. It was"—I clenched my fists and frowned. I had to get this right—"unthinkable before I met you."

He crossed the room and sat beside me on the fireplace hearth, and when I touched his knee, he did not pull away. "Holy shit!" He noticed the red blisters that had appeared on my hands over the past two days. "What happened to you?"

He didn't know. He still thought his journal had burned in the fire. I pulled it from my back pocket where I had been carrying it and held it out to him. "I meant to give it back to you that night in the forest, but you were so upset and then we…well, we had other things on our minds. And then you wouldn't talk to me and then—"

"Please stop saying *and then.*" He took the journal from me and ran his hand over the blackened cover, his fingers coming away with flakes of ash clinging to them. He traced the inward curves where the fire had feasted on it, the jagged edges crumbling and falling on his legs. "Jake threw it in the fire and you"—he shook his head—"you saved it? Everybody had to know I'd been writing about you. Why? Why would you do that? If you care that much, why did you run out on me?"

Finally, a chance to tell him. "I wasn't running away from you, Ian. I was running away from me."

He leaned forward, the journal clutched in his hands, and exhaled. "Yeah, I get that."

"So you'll forgive me?" I asked and immediately wished I hadn't. It sounded too pushy. Too hopeful.

He turned to look at me, his eyes glistening in the firelight. "I'm going to try, Jonathan. I'm really going to try."

❖

The storm raged for hours. Ian curled up on the braided rug in front of the smoldering fire and fought sleep. My chest hurt from trying to keep my feelings inside.

He rolled on his back and threw an arm over his head, smiling in his sleep. The glowing embers cast long shadows against the log walls and his face, revealing a peacefulness I'd never seen there before. The room darkened into a charcoal wash.

"That's what he meant." I didn't mean to speak out loud.

"Hmm?" Ian mumbled. "What who meant?"

"It doesn't matter. Go back to sleep. I'm sorry I woke you."

Ian opened his eyes and looked at me. "No, it's okay. Tell me."

"It's just something Simon said that didn't make sense. He told me to see the light, not just look for it."

He sat up, yawning. "Sounds very Simon-esque."

I laughed. "Tell me about it. But he was right. I won't find light by looking directly into it. It just burns my retinas and leaves me with blind spots. No, I have to look at the place where the light falls. That's where it is."

"Where what is?" Amber light played across his face as he smiled at me again.

"Everything, Ian. Everything."

Chapter Twenty-six

Ian snuck out of the cabin when the rain still fell, but the lightning and thunder had died away. He thought it best if we didn't walk into camp together. Even though I wished I didn't, I agreed with him.

"It's the last day. Only a few more hours and then you never have to see this place again," he said, glimpsing only some of my feelings.

The first rays of tentative pink streaked across the sky when Dawn, carrying crutches, and Bear approached the cabin. I could feel Dawn's shadow as it moved into the room. She studied me from the doorway, seeing things I could never express.

"I have to go back, don't I?"

"Eventually, but not right this minute. For now I think you should let me adjust your crutches."

"Thanks." I stood and she adjusted the crutches to my height.

"Do your armpits a favor and don't lean all your weight on them. Just use them for balance, okay?"

"Okay."

"Now sit while I make us some breakfast."

I sat in Dawn's old, comfortable plaid chair and inhaled the dust that rose from the stale ash of last night's fire. Bear stretched and looked me in the eye. He picked up a slimy and well-chewed nub of what was once a rawhide bone and dropped the sticky gift on my leg. Drool dangled from his mouth and landed on my pants.

"Aw, thanks, Bear. I bet that's your favorite bone." I scratched under his chin, which must have felt good because he leaned forward and buried his head in my lap. Dawn moved around her small kitchen. Cabinet and refrigerator doors opened and closed, pans clattered, a whisk stirred something in a bowl. The air filled with smells that set my stomach grumbling. She returned with a steaming mug and a plate of scrambled eggs.

"Drink. And eat some eggs."

I held the stoneware mug to my face and inhaled the soothing scent of orange and clove. I took a sip and warmth spread throughout my body. The dread retreated just a bit. "Mmm, what is it?"

"It's a special tea that has healing properties."

"Did your mother teach you how to make it?" I imagined an older Native American woman with long braids crushing herbs in a clay pot.

"No, Hannah did." Dawn crossed to the window and opened it. A fresh morning breeze circulated through the room. All the scents of danger that had filled the air the night before had disappeared.

"She did?" I put the mug on the table, uncertain whether or not I wanted anything from Hannah or the world she represented anymore. I picked up a fork and stabbed some eggs. I held them to my mouth, but the smell nauseated me. Dawn caught my eyes and I shoved them in my mouth anyway.

"Yes, I showed up one night at Paul and Hannah's cabin, looking pretty much as crappy as you do right now. Hannah made me a cup of that tea, and Paul prayed with me. I found out that my world was okay after all."

"Paul said awful things to me." The anger and accusation in my voice surprised even me.

"I'm listening." Dawn sat on the hearth.

"I didn't choose this. And I'm not under satanic attack or in bondage to sin. This is just who I am, Dawn, and I can't pretend to be someone I'm not anymore, but Paul's never going to accept that." For the second time in a month, I cried with Dawn. She sat with me until I could speak again. Outside, a chainsaw sprang to life. Bear cocked his head to listen. "And neither will my parents."

"You're probably right."

"So you know? About me? That I'm—" I couldn't say the word aloud again.

"That you're strong and filled with courage and that you have begun a vision quest? Yes, I guessed that."

"I've begun a what?"

"A vision quest. It means that you have begun asking questions about your life. More importantly, it means that you have begun to search for your own answers. My people have a saying. *No man begins to be until he has seen his vision.* The Ojibwe believe that *Gichi-manidoo* will show you the answers you are looking for when you are ready."

"But I'm ready now!" My voice sounded desperate, even to me.

"You know enough about God to know that our timing is not His timing."

"Yeah, but Dawn, you don't understand. My mother is coming today. I don't know how I'm going to face her." The chainsaw chewed into something that resisted. The humming rose higher until it squealed.

"You're wrong. I understand better than you know." Dawn rose and walked into her bedroom. She returned with a picture of a woman with olive skin and black eyes. The family resemblance was unmistakable.

"Your mother?"

"Yes. I haven't seen her in four years." Dawn traced her mother's face with her finger.

"Why?"

"I came here as a part of an ecology class. What I found changed my life, but not right away. I went back to my college life of studying and partying, but inside, I felt empty. I returned to the reservation that summer. I thought being with my family would fill the hole that grew bigger every day, but it didn't. So one night, four years ago, I just left. I climbed in my car and drove back here. It was crazy. I mean, I barely knew these people, but they had something I needed. It was the middle of the night when I knocked on Paul and Hannah's door. He took one look at my face and asked if he could pray with me. I don't even think I realized that I had begun my vision quest. I just knew that I was hurting, but that night, as Paul prayed, I received my vision. I saw the face of *Gichi-manidoo*, and it was Jesus Christ. I saw that He loves me more than I could ever imagine being loved. I am a Native American woman who loves Jesus Christ. This is my path, and it gives me such joy to walk it. The only sadness is how it hurts my mother. In her opinion, I turned my back on my people."

I pictured Paul and Hannah opening their doors and their hearts to Dawn and couldn't help but smile to think of Hannah brewing her special tea and Paul with his head bent in prayer, leading Dawn to Christ. But my smile faded when I pictured Ian and me standing outside a closed door that would never open as long as we were together.

"Are you angry with your mother?"

"I was. For a long time." The chainsaw broke through the resistance and died down to a steady buzz. The sound of some huge thing thudding to the ground startled me, and I jumped in my chair.

"But not anymore?"

"No, not anymore. The more I gave my heart to Christ, the more He filled it with love until there just wasn't room for anger." She gazed out her window. The air blew across her face. The turquoise beads she wore in her long hair clattered against each other like a living wind chime. "Besides, she has a good heart. In time, my mother will soften. As will yours. But now, I need to go check on the loons." Dawn stood.

"Do you think they made it through the storm?"

"Edward and Bella probably did. Most likely they flew away when the storm hit, but the babies were just weeks old. Too young to fly."

"I'm so sorry." I stood to leave. Bear barked his disappointment. "I won't be coming back next summer, Dawn."

"I know, but we will see each other again." Dawn tilted her head, listening to the wind. "I am proud of you, *Needjee*. Go in peace, Jonathan Cooper."

Chapter Twenty-seven

The Loon's Nest had been burglarized. At least, it looked that way. Plastic mattresses lay bare. Damp, musty towels hung from every surface, their deadline for drying quickly approaching. Suitcases and duffel bags were open, half-packed, and a stream of worn socks and underwear cluttered the floor. Sleeping bags were badly rolled up and waited to unravel. The mosquito population of northern Minnesota could relax; Bryan's bug zapper was nowhere to be seen. Jake was the only person who was completely packed. Either he was in a hurry to get home, which I doubted, or he didn't want his mom or dad to pry into his bags stuffed with his Iron Man pj's and his porn. I could even see the outline of the magazines at the bottom of his duffel bag if I looked closely. Lucky for Jake, his parents probably wouldn't.

It was a relief to have the cabin to myself as I packed up. Everyone else was either checking out the damage from the storm or waiting for parents to arrive.

Rolling up my sleeping bag proved too difficult while balancing on crutches, so I left it. Mom and I could figure it out later, after the closing-day activities. I stood outside and listened to the hum of Spirit Lake in the distance, breathed in the fresh pine air, and looked at the cabin. When had the paint peeled from the windowsills? How had I never noticed the torn screen before?

Without looking back, I turned and hobbled away.

Warrior's Way should have been renamed Wounded Warrior's Way. I limped over the campground, my eyes wandering across the forest of fir and birch and the eternal blue of the passive lake that rolled toward the beach in the aftermath of the night's storm. Trees were uprooted. Half the roof was missing from the canteen. Garbage was strewn over the campground I no longer recognized. The fire pit at the bonfire had turned into a pool of ashes.

My breath caught in my throat. The willow tree, guardian of Spirit Lake Bible Camp, lay on the ground, charred and split in two. Half of its body was twisted and gnarled and lay defeated on the sandy beach. Cruel black streaks along the fallen limb gave evidence of the violence it had suffered. The other half, only lightly blackened, reached toward Heaven as if it had died in the middle of a prayer. My throat swelled shut and burned with grief. I tried to swallow and couldn't. I let my body's weight rest on my crutches as Sean bent over the fallen willow with a chainsaw, dismembering the remains. The wind shifted, and I choked on the wood dust that swirled around me like cremated ashes being scattered.

"Jonathan, I've been looking for you. I heard you were hurt. Are you okay? What happened?" Bethany walked up to join me.

"I sprained my ankle. It's no big deal."

"No big deal? You were so brave, going back into the storm last night."

"Thanks, but you know what the flip side of bravery is, don't you?"

"No. What is it?"

"Stupidity." We laughed together and, for a moment, it almost felt right. "Lightning?" I guessed, looking at the fallen willow.

"Yeah, I saw it get hit. The storm rolled in off the lake, and the whole sky turned this awful shade of green when a line of white streaked through the sky and hit the willow tree. All the lights went out in the lodge, so Paul made us go into the basement, and I didn't see anything else." I remembered a flash of light and a dead phone in Ian's hand as he had called out to Paul.

"So, it seems that a month goes by quicker than I thought." Bethany avoided my eyes.

"You must be excited about seeing your family again today." The chainsaw sprang to life, and Sean began carving into the half of the willow that still stood. Nothing would be allowed to remain.

"I guess. Actually, I'm not sure I'm ready to go home. It's been nice just being Bethany, you know."

"Yeah, I do know. I'm not ready for parents' day either." The ticking of the clock that had been growing stronger for days had become deafening. It drowned out the whining chainsaw and the screaming tree and the soft-spoken girl.

"So, I found your flowers and note with your phone number on my bunk. That was so sweet of you. I'd love for us to stay in touch too. Here." Bethany handed me a piece of paper. "It's my phone number. My mother won't let me call boys, and I don't have a cell, but you can call my home number. Don't leave a message with one of my brothers or sisters though. I won't get it for sure." The largest remaining limb from the willow tree surrendered and crashed to the ground. Sean repositioned the chainsaw and began attacking the split trunk. I stared at the small piece of paper and said nothing.

"So, I'll see you in Curtain Call for our performance, then."

"Yeah, sure, Bethany. I'll be there." It would have been so much easier to follow that path. She was everything I was supposed to have chosen.

"Okay, later." Bethany walked away, and suddenly I knew I couldn't mislead her.

"Ah, Bethany."

She turned to look at me. "What is it?" Her face lit up.

"The flowers and note didn't come from me." I hated hurting her.

"You didn't write this?" She took another handwritten note from her pocket and gave it to me. *Bethany, it was cool spending time with you in Curtain Call. Give me a call sometime.* The only signature was one letter *J* followed by a phone number.

"No, I'm sorry. I didn't write that."

Disappointment, then understanding crossed her face. "But then, it must have been written by…"

"I'm sorry, Bethany. I never meant to hurt you."

She smiled. "It was always Ian, wasn't it?"

"Since the moment I saw him."

Bethany nodded and walked away. This time, I let her go and she did not look back.

The chainsaw finally stopped. I filled my lungs with as much pine-scented sorrow as I could stand. Exhaling, I said good-bye to the willow tree, to Spirit Lake Bible Camp, to the people here who were like family, and to the Jonathan I had tried so hard to be. The back of my throat burned from holding back my tears. In the distance I saw Ian, standing by Sara and Lily on the stage of the outdoor theater. They were maneuvering the TV stand into place. He wore a suit and tie, and his red hair was slicked back. He looked exactly like a news anchor. I would have laughed had my heart not been breaking.

A steady line of cars streamed down the dirt road that led toward Spirit Lake Bible Camp. Parents' day had begun.

Chapter Twenty-eight

Hey, Jonathan!" Simon's voice reached me from the arts-and-crafts pavilion. "Look at you cruise on those crutches. Got a moment?"

"Absolutely." I lurched over to where he sat, saturated in the scent of turpentine as he cleaned the paintbrushes and tidied up for the end of the summer session. I had been hoping for a chance to say good-bye. He had been so much more than a counselor. More than an art teacher. He had become my friend. The easel held a completed portrait of a dark-haired woman, strong and fierce, dancing in the lush forest. The dawning sun was breaking over the ridge of trees. Her white flowing dress fanned out around her bare legs like an orchid opening to the morning light.

"Oh, Simon, it's fantastic."

"Thank you. I call it *Morning Dance.*" He smiled and ran his hand over the canvas.

"It's beautiful, Simon. I saw it. Last night when the shadows played across Ian's face, I understood. All this time I've been looking right into the light, measuring its strength, but I should have been looking at where it fell. Like the picture of my mom."

"The light shows us truth. Sometimes it shows us more than we want to see. That's what happened with that picture, isn't it?"

"Yeah, I wanted to take a peaceful picture of her. I suppose because that's how I want her to be. Instead, the picture showed her looking worried because that's how she really is."

He smiled. "I knew you'd see it. Believe me, there are a lot of people who never do. Did you figure out anything about the shadows?"

I thought of the dark shadow that fell across my mother's face. The softening I had seen on Ian's face. "This may sound weird, but I think the light asks the questions, and the shadows give us the answers."

"You've begun to see the shades of gray. I can't believe how far you've come. You're going to be an amazing photographer someday." Simon looked at me. Artist to artist.

"Thank you for speaking up for me last night."

Simon sloshed the brushes one final time in the turpentine and set them on a table to dry. I looked around the supply hut and realized that the shelves were empty. Everything had been packed up. A prickling feeling traveled over my skin.

"What happened, Simon? After I left the lodge?"

He dried his hands on a paper towel. "Paul and I had a long talk."

"You mean Paul fired you."

"Let's say we both realized our philosophies have grown too far apart." I heard the sadness in his voice. "Now before you go blaming yourself, you should know that this has been a long time coming. Throughout the years I've known Paul, he has become more conservative in his beliefs while mine have been broadening. This day was unavoidable."

I still felt guilty. "Black and white versus shades of gray."

"Exactly." Simon smiled at me.

"What are you going to do now, Simon?"

"*Remember ye not the former things, neither consider the things of old. Behold, I will do a new thing; now it shall spring forth; shall ye not know it? I will even make a way in the wilderness, and rivers in the desert.*" Simon quoted the Bible. "Isaiah 43:18 and 19. I have no idea what I'm going to do now, Jonathan, but I know that God will do a new thing with my life. He will make a way."

The willow tree was gone. The cross, scarred with Ian's footprints, had survived. Simon was leaving, but Paul would remain. Spirit Lake Bible Camp would go on, to be certain, but as far as I was concerned, it could go on without me.

"It still feels like my fault. You wouldn't have argued with Paul if I hadn't insisted on going to find Ian. And guess what? He was fine. In the end, he rescued me." I grimaced.

"So I heard, but that's exactly how relationships are supposed to work." Simon smiled. "Two people loving each other, helping each other." He looked toward the cabin at the edge of the forest. Honking horns came from the direction of the parking lot.

"A relationship with Ian—what a weird thought." Saying it aloud made me dizzy.

"But does it feel right?"

"Sometimes, I think yeah, it could. If he's able to forgive me, that is. But then I think about my mom. I know how she's going to feel about this. And my dad, well, you've met him."

He read the look of panic that passed over my face. "Right. Sergeant Cooper. Look, I'm not saying it's going to be easy. You're going to have to give them time and try to remember that they love you. Believe it or not, I think your dad would have been proud of you when you went back into the storm for Ian. You should have seen yourself. The way you stood up to Paul and walked into that storm, determined to find Ian. You were a soldier last night, even if it does take some time for your dad to see it that way. As far as whether or not Ian forgives you, well…whatever he decides to do won't change who you are. You know that, right?"

"Yeah, I do. I finally know who I am."

Simon smiled at me as he wheeled over to his workbench and picked up a piece of paper with a phone number written on it.

"That's my cell. I want you to call me, anytime, okay? You are not alone."

More tears sprang to my eyes, though I would have thought I'd run dry. I had never cried so much in my life. There were things I wanted to tell him, but the pavilion spun. I nodded, unable to talk.

"Now go, find your mom. Look her in the eye and be yourself." Simon squared his shoulders. "As for me, I think it's time I took my own advice." He winked at me. "Wish me luck."

"Woo-hoo! You go get her!"

Simon wheeled toward the small cabin at the edge of the forest while I took one last look around the arts-and-crafts pavilion and tucked Simon's phone number into my empty pocket. All the gold coins had finally been spent.

Chapter Twenty-nine

The pit in my stomach grew bigger as car after car turned into the parking lot. *She's late?* The thought shocked me. I choked on the stifling stench of exhaust that poured out of idling cars. The door to the administration building opened and Mom walked out with Paul. She held a Kleenex to her eyes. *Oh crap, she's early.*

"I don't understand, Paul. How could this happen? What am I supposed to do now?" Her voice carried across the parking lot and pierced me through the heart.

"I've given you a list of Christian counselors I know in the Cities." Paul's voice soothed. "They'll help you. Linda, please don't hesitate to call me anytime."

My mom stared at me.

You're the man of the house now, Jon. Take care of your mother. My chest tightened.

"Jon!" She looked pale, shaken. "Look at you on crutches! Oh dear Lord, what has happened to you?"

I knew she was asking about more than my ankle.

She crossed the parking lot to where I stood, leaning on my crutches. Her arms rose to give me a hug, but I saw her hesitation and she saw mine. She dropped them to her side and stood in front of me.

"Hi, Mom," I said. "I'm going to be fine. It's just a sprain."

"We should leave. I think we should go. Now."

"I'm in Curtain Call, Mom. Sara's counting on me. Can't we leave right after the play?"

She hesitated, then nodded.

I breathed a sigh of relief as I walked her toward the outdoor theater.

❖

"It's about time you showed up." Sara looked stressed as she fastened the belt of chiming bells around Bethany's waist. "Everyone's here. We're almost ready to begin."

"Sorry, Sara, I'm not moving too fast." I apologized and ducked into the dimly lit costume hut. I breathed in the air, thickened with years of dust, and threw my purple robe over my T-shirt and shorts. The color of royalty, according to Lily. I attached a realistic-looking black beard and looked for my crown where I'd left it, but it wasn't there. In fact, it wasn't anywhere in the costume hut. I gave up and took a look at myself in the mirror. Herod on crutches. Minus his crown. Why not? A sharp rap at the door cut short my reflections.

"Jonathan? You in there?" Ian's voice was an answer to prayer. "Let me in, quick. Before someone sees." I pushed the door open. He slipped in without anyone spotting him.

"Listen, this is it. I don't think we're going to get another chance to say good-bye." Ian looked ridiculously cute with his slicked-back hair. "My foster parents know. Paul asked them to come up early so they could talk." Sounds of murmuring audience voices and tinkling bells carried through the walls along with the muted tones of Aaron's guitar as he provided some entertainment before the play.

"Looking fine, girl!" Jake's voice boomed out behind the stage, too loud to earn him any points with Sara, though maybe with Bethany.

"Yeah, my mom knows too. She looks like she's going to throw up." I imagined her sitting, head whirling, in a sea of happy faces. My heart hurt for her. "Ian—"

He shushed me. "Look, what you did was bullshit, but I think I understand why you freaked out." He avoided my eyes.

"Does that mean you forgive me?"

"I don't feel right leaving things the way they are. Let's say I'm willing to let it go."

"I'll take it." I pulled him into my arms, and he lifted his face to me.

Our lips touched awkwardly. Our noses bumped. Though we'd kissed before, this kiss tasted different. It tasted of good-bye.

"Ian." I mouthed his name. His eyes fluttered open. "What happens next?"

"Maybe it will be easier now that they know. We won't have to hide. Maybe they'll understand." Ian sounded so hopeful.

"I don't think so, but it's a nice thought."

"It's only two more years, right? And then college. Besides, I'm going to come and visit you this fall. We're going to go to the Guthrie and take in a play. And you're going to take me to the bookstore near your house." The clinking of water glasses and *oohs* and *aahs* told me that Lily and Hannah were moving through the tables, providing our dinner guests with their meals.

He didn't know my parents. "Um—"

"No, Jonathan. Don't. I need to imagine this. It's the only way I can say good-bye to you."

"Okay, I get it. And then I'm going to take you to a coffee shop I know and we can have strawberry-rhubarb pie."

"Only if I can have a whole pie for myself." He grinned, remembering.

"You can have anything you want. I'll make sure of it." I reached for him and pulled him into my arms again. He knocked over one of my crutches and it clattered to the ground.

"And we can work on our coffee-table book." Ian laughed as he knelt and handed me the crutch. The situation was ridiculous, but my laughter sounded wrong, given what I was feeling.

"I don't think there are many porcupines in Minnetonka."

"That's okay. We'll figure something out." I heard the layers of meaning behind his words. "Two years. That's not so long," Ian whispered.

A sharp rap on the door shattered the fragile dream. "Jonathan, five minutes!" Sara said.

"Coming!" I dropped my voice and whispered to Ian, "What are we going to do? We can't both walk out of here."

"It's okay. I'm not in scene one. Just the video of me. I'll wait in here until the play begins, and then I'll sneak out. You'd better go now."

I stood with my hand on the doorknob and searched his eyes where I found my reason to take the next step along my vision quest. "I'll find a way to see you again. I promise."

"I know you will. Now get out there. Everybody's waiting for the star of Curtain Call. I'd tell you to break a leg, but…"

There was the grin I loved. Flecks of dust danced in the golden light as Ian stood, surrounded by twenty years of moth-eaten costumes and handmade props.

"That's too bad," I said, wishing I could freeze time and never leave him or the safety of this hut. "All they're going to get is me. I'm done acting."

Because part of me demanded more: the right to walk hand in hand with him in the sunshine for everyone to see.

Nothing less would be enough.

Chapter Thirty

Backstage, Lily held my crown out to me. "I found it on top of the bust of Ian's head with a piece of paper taped to it that read *King of the Fags.* I told our executioner that if he pulled another stunt like that I'd take his head myself." She sent a withering glance at Jake, who was annoying the hell out of Bethany by swinging his ax at her. Idiot needed to enroll in Flirting 101.

"You did not." My mouth dropped open.

"I most certainly did." She reached up to straighten my beard. "Hate is hate. I don't care what anyone says."

"Lily, you are beautiful." I leaned over and kissed her on the cheek.

"And you're brave. I wanted to tell you that." She blushed.

I stood there, basking in the warmth of her words and the sound of Aaron's guitar music. The audience appeared to be enjoying Ian's idea of dinner theater as they nibbled Hannah's bread and drank their wine. Mom, sitting in the front row, took a sip and sniffed her glass.

"Ah, Lily, did anyone help you set the tables?"

"Yeah, Jake and Bryan poured the grape juice while I filled the bread baskets."

"You're kidding me!"

"Why? What's wrong?" Lily turned to look at the audience, worry written across her face.

"Nothing. Just remember, when Paul asks you about the wine, you only filled the bread baskets. Got it?"

"Got it. Are Jake and Bryan in trouble?" A grin spread across her face.

"Oh yeah." I chuckled, enjoying the scene that played out in my mind. "Trouble of epic proportions."

Things went uphill or downhill from there, depending on your perspective. For me it was one big roller-coaster ride. Smooth all the way up through act 1 and act 2 until we hit Salome's seductive dance that contained more lurching and leaping than bumping and grinding.

"I was horrible!" Bethany wailed backstage as the audience watched Ian's television broadcast cut to static, an indication that John the Baptist had been arrested.

"No, you weren't. You were sexy," I said, relying on kindness and not first-hand knowledge to sound convincing.

"You're not doing her any favors, you know." MacKenzie slathered on another layer of plumping lipstick. "Let her learn from her failures. It's the only way she'll improve."

Jake looked murderous, which was perfect considering he was going to chop off John the Baptist's head in the next scene. Just thinking about it made me twitchy.

"Shut up, MacKenzie!" Jake growled. "Bethany, you were beautiful and classy. Not everyone can pull that off." Bethany smiled at Jake like she was seeing him for the first time.

Oh, goody. A socially approved happily ever after for Jake and Bethany. I tried and failed to keep my resentment to a minimum, and then MacKenzie yanked Bethany and me out of our pity parties and onto the stage.

"Did Salome's dance please you, my king?" MacKenzie, as Queen Herodias, addressed the audience. I coughed to remind her that I was sitting behind her at the dinner table, supposedly celebrating and drinking heavily.

"Yes, my queen. Very much." I picked up a goblet, took a deep drink, and swore under my breath. Of course Jake and Bryan had filled *my* glass with actual grape juice. The douche nozzles. I could have used a little liquid strength, given what I knew was coming. "So much that I would like to thank the lovely Salome by granting her any request." I swayed forward and grabbed the table, partly because I was supposed to be drunk and partly because I felt sick. I hated this scene.

MacKenzie flipped her hair and swayed her hips as she sauntered over to Bethany and whispered in her ear. I hated to admit it, but she did embody the haughty Queen Herodias.

"Come, Salome," I said to Bethany. "Surely you must have one request from your king?"

MacKenzie nudged Bethany, who stumbled forward, looking every bit the manipulated daughter.

"Yes, King Herod, if I may…" Bethany turned to look at MacKenzie for reassurance, and even I couldn't tell if she was acting or not. MacKenzie nodded and Bethany continued. "I would like to request peace for you. Freedom from the lies that are spread about you."

"You ask for my own heart's desires," I said, glancing at my mother in the front row. She looked away and took a long drink from her glass. "How may I grant this request?"

"You must silence the one who slanders you, my king." Bethany's voice rang out over the stage, across the audience, over all of Spirit Lake Bible Camp and beyond. "Bring me John the Baptist's head on a platter!"

I knew my next line. Of course, I did. *Make it so.* Just three little words. Three little words that would haul Ian, bound and humiliated, onto the stage. Three little words that would summon Jake to drag him sobbing off the stage where the audience would hear him scream and imagine an ax falling. Three little words that stuck in my throat and refused to be spoken.

Seconds of silence on stage are minutes. Hours. Decades. A lifetime.

MacKenzie glared at me, willing me to speak.

I did not. Could not.

I leaned my head on the table and closed my eyes, shutting out all the staring faces.

MacKenzie spoke again, groping for words never written by Sara. "*Hello!* Did you hear her?" She improvised. Badly. "Are you going to order the scum's execution or not?"

It might have been the darkness that surrounded me, reminding me of prayers and dreams and the world beneath the surface of Spirit Lake where his arms had once turned gentle. Maybe it was her calling him scum.

I stood and faced her, faced them all. "I will not! You will not force me to betray a good man!"

Offstage, Sara gasped. Ian laughed. The metal tray clattered to the ground. I turned toward the sounds and saw Lily and Kari scrambling after the bust of Ian's head as it rolled toward the stage. Lily grabbed it just in time.

MacKenzie swiveled and looked at Sara. "What do we do now?" she asked, shattering the illusion of the play and her reputation as a consummate actress. Bethany didn't wait for Sara's answer and bolted from the stage. MacKenzie followed her, leaving me alone to deal with the fallout.

I stared at the bewildered faces of the audience and had no panic. No fear. No clue what to say.

And then he walked onto the stage. Ian, his tie crooked and his slick newscaster hair jutting out in crazy angles because he was supposed to look as if he'd been roughed up for this scene. Everything about him said he was a defeated man. Everything, except his face.

Ian strode center stage, the prop microphone with the letters *CESR* in his hands, and addressed the audience. "We interrupt this program to bring you a breaking news story. A good man chose love and not hate. Why that is newsworthy, I'll never know, but it does secure ratings and that means job security. You may now return to your regularly scheduled lives, hopefully changed for the better."

He bowed and exited stage left.

Like I said, it was a roller-coaster ride marked by twists and turns. Oh, and ear-shattering screams too. A few from Sara. Most from MacKenzie.

CHAPTER THIRTY-ONE

The ride home was quiet. I sat in the passenger seat and replayed my last hour at camp: Dawn and Simon clapping and beaming as Ian and I walked onto the stage, held hands, and bowed for our curtain call. Paul hauling Jake and Bryan along with their parents into the admin building, an empty bottle of Manischewitz in his hand. The painful fact that Ian had been right—we had not been given another chance at good-bye.

"The play was, erm, original." My mother stared straight ahead, white knuckled as she clutched the steering wheel. "You were wonderful in it, as always."

"Thanks, Mom."

"Do you think you'll be in Curtain Call next year when you're a junior counselor?"

"I highly doubt it." The road thumped beneath our car's tires as mile after mile disappeared behind us, taking me farther and farther away from Spirit Lake Bible Camp.

"It's such a blessing that storm didn't do any real damage. Imagine if the lodge had been hit by lightning."

"Yeah, I guess." I remembered the fallen willow.

"Oh, Jon, I forgot. Simon asked me to give you this." She pointed behind her where a package, wrapped in hand-painted paper, sat on the backseat. "He said you forgot it at the arts-and-crafts pavilion."

"Jonathan, Mom. My name is *Jonathan*." My voice sounded harsh even to me as I reached into the backseat and got the gift.

"Of course, Jonathan, if that's what you want. You look so tired. Is there anything you want to talk about?"

I tore open the wrapping and gasped when I found the statue of the willow tree, a note tied to one of the branches.

Jonathan, may you remember what you loved most about Spirit Lake.

P.S. The answer is a relationship with you, just as you are. That is what God wants most from you.

Like the fallen willow, I couldn't weep any more. I had finally run dry.

"Jonathan?" she pressed.

I rewound back to her original question. "No, not really."

I knew she wouldn't push it. I knew her discomfort would give me space. In fact, I was counting on it. Silence fell between us and I concentrated on the view from my window. Signs for Split Rock Lighthouse and Gooseberry Falls sped past us. I was about to suggest we grab a slice at Betty's Pies when the steering wheel turned in my mother's hands and we pulled into the parking lot of Flood Bay State Wayside Scenic Overlook off Highway 61. Mom shifted the car into park and the engine sputtered and died. Lake Superior spread out before us, enormous, filling the entire windshield of the car with its endless expanse of blue.

"We're stopping?" I looked sideways at her in surprise. Her hands hung relaxed on the steering wheel. Color returned to her knuckles, but her shoulders sagged.

"We always stop here to say good-bye to Lake Superior. It's our tradition. Why wouldn't we this year?"

Oh, I don't know, I wanted to say. *I thought that since everything else had changed, this would too.* But we didn't do direct in my family. We spoke through veils and relied on each other's faces to tell the truth. The car dinged as Mom opened her door. A breeze, cool and fresh off the lake, rushed in to greet me. Mom walked over to one of the low, flat rocks and sat, her face turned away from me and into the wind as she stared across Lake Superior. I opened my door and hopped on my one good leg to the back of the car. Reaching into the backseat, I grabbed my crutches and made my way toward her. Somewhere, deep inside, I had always known the day would come when my truth would surface. When she would finally know that our stories were separate, hers and mine. She and my father would live their lives, sometimes together and sometimes apart. Each following truth, her God and his country, in their white house with the black shutters and a cranberry door.

There was space on the rock beside her, but I hesitated. Uncertain. A stirring of wind like a soft breath blew again off the infinite lake, carrying with it the sound of pulsing waves, constant as a heartbeat. I imagined the indiscernible shore, far off to be certain, but real and calling to me. The day was fast approaching, I knew, when my journey would require more than half a story with a slanted roof.

I looked at my mother and my palms grew moist. My chest seized. Would I lose her along the way?

"I'm sorry," I said. "I don't want to hurt you."

The fingers on her right hand played with her gold wedding ring. It spun easily on her thin left ring finger. Around and around, with no sign of ceasing.

"I know you don't." Her words were small and quiet.

I barely heard them and yet I clung to them, my hope dangling like a rock climber scaling a sheer cliff. There were so many things I wanted to say. So much I needed to explain, but now wasn't the time. Words spoken too soon, I knew, could be wounding. Besides, I was still waiting for the words to surface, so I could tell myself the story of the past four weeks. She stood and took a final look at Lake Superior, turned and walked toward our car.

My hand slipped on the handhold of my crutch. Pain shot into my shoulder as my weight crashed down on my armpit. Tears sprang to my eyes. *Behold, I will do a new thing.* I felt the familiar quickening of my soul. I took a deep, calming breath and looked at the lake, endless in its possibilities.

"Thank you, God, for loving me just as I am." I turned and hobbled after her.

On the road again, I pressed my cheek against the cool glass of the car window. My golden month of independence was over and a new season of—what? I didn't know—was about to begin. I only knew one thing for certain. The guy, reflected in my window, was no longer a stranger. We weren't best of friends yet, but I admired something about him. He had guts.

It was a start.

We drove into Two Harbors. Familiar landmarks sped by: Lou's Motel and Fish House, Judy's Café, the Vanilla Bean Café, and the Blueberry House.

"We're making good time," my mother said.

I looked at my iPhone. *I have bars! Finally.* It took seconds to access my Facebook account. *Ian McGuire,* I typed in the search box and hit enter. I should have expected the profile picture, an image of a writing quill and a bottle of ink, and yet I felt disappointed. I already missed his face.

My finger hovered for a moment.

Request sent, the iPhone screen read.

About the Author

Minnesota writer Juliann Rich spent her childhood in search of the perfect climbing tree. The taller the better! A branch thirty feet off the ground and surrounded by leaves, caterpillars, birds, and squirrels was a good perch for a young girl to find herself. Seeking truth in nature and finding a unique point of view remain crucial elements in her life as well as her writing.

Juliann is a PFLAG mom who can be found walking Pride parades with her son. She is also the daughter of evangelical Christian parents. As such, she has been caught in the crossfire of the most heated topic to challenge our society and our churches today. She is drawn to stories that shed light on the conflicts that arise when sexual orientation, spirituality, family dynamics, and peer relationships collide. You can read more about her journey as an author and as an affirming mom on her website, www.juliannrich.com and her blog, www.therainbowtreeblog.com.

Juliann lives with her husband and their two dogs, Mr. Sherlock Holmes and Ms. Bella Moriarty, in the beautiful Minnesota River Valley.

Soliloquy Titles From Bold Strokes Books

Caught in the Crossfire by Juliann Rich. Two boys at Bible camp; one forbidden love. (978-1-62639-070-6)

Remember Me by Melanie Batchelor. After a tragic event occurs, teenager Jamie Richards is left questioning the identity of the girl she loved, Erica Sinclair. (978-1-62639-184-0)

Frenemy of the People by Nora Olsen. Clarissa and Lexie have despised each other as long as they can remember, but when they both find themselves helping an unlikely contender for homecoming queen, they are catapulted into an unexpected romance. (978-1-62639-063-8)

The Balance by Neal Wooten. Love and survival come together in the distant future as Piri and Niko faceoff against the worst factions of mankind's evolution. (978-1-62639-055-3)

The Unwanted by Jeffrey Ricker. Jamie Thomas is plunged into danger when he discovers his mother is an Amazon who needs his help to save the tribe from a vengeful god. (978-1-62639-048-5)

Because of Her by KE Payne. When Tabby Morton is forced to move to London, she's convinced her life will never be the same again. But the beautiful and intriguing Eden Palmer is about to show her that this time, change is most definitely for the better. (978-1-62639-049-2)

Asher's Fault by Elizabeth Wheeler. Fourteen-year-old Asher Price sees the world in black and white, much like the photos he takes, but when his little brother drowns at the same moment Asher experiences his first same-sex kiss, he can no longer hide behind the lens of his camera and eventually discovers he isn't the only one with a secret. (978-1-60282-982-4)

The Seventh Pleiade by Andrew J. Peters. When Atlantis is besieged by violent storms, tremors, and a barbarian army, it will be up to a young gay prince to find a way for the kingdom's survival. (978-1-60282-960-2)

The Missing Juliet: A Fisher Key Adventure by Sam Cameron. A teenage detective and her friends search for a kidnapped Hollywood star in the Florida Keys. (978-1-60282-959-6)

Meeting Chance by Jennifer Lavoie. When man's best friend turns on Aaron Cassidy, the teen keeps his distance until fate puts Chance in his hands. (978-1-60282-952-7)

Lake Thirteen by Greg Herren. A visit to an old cemetery seems like fun to a group of five teenagers, who soon learn that sometimes it's best to leave old ghosts alone. (978-1-60282-894-0)

The Road to Her by KE Payne. Sparks fly when actress Holly Croft, star of UK soap *Portobello Road*, meets her new on-screen love interest, the enigmatic and sexy Elise Manford. (978-1-60282-887-2)

Swans and Klons by Nora Olsen. In a future world where there are no males, sixteen-year-old Rubric and her girlfriend Salmon Jo must fight to survive when everything they believed in turns out to be a lie. (978-1-60282-874-2)

Kings of Ruin by Sam Cameron. High school student Danny Kelly and loner Kevin Clark must team up to defeat a top-secret alien intelligence that likes to wreak havoc with fiery car, truck, and train accidents. (978-1-60282-864-3)

Wonderland by David-Matthew Barnes. After her mother's sudden death, Destiny Moore is sent to live with her two gay uncles on Avalon Cove, a mysterious island on which she uncovers a secret place called Wonderland, where love and magic prove to be real. (978-1-60282-788-2)

Another 365 Days by KE Payne. Clemmie Atkins is back, and her life is more complicated than ever! Still madly in love with her girlfriend, Clemmie suddenly finds her life turned upside down with distractions, confessions, and the return of a familiar face… (978-1-60282-775-2)

The Secret of Othello by Sam Cameron. Florida teen detectives Steven and Denny risk their lives to search for a sunken NASA satellite—but under the waves, no one can hear you scream… (978-1-60282-742-4)

Andy Squared by Jennifer Lavoie. Andrew never thought anyone could come between him and his twin sister, Andrea…until Ryder rode into town. (978-1-60282-743-1)

Sara by Greg Herren. A mysterious and beautiful new student at Southern Heights High School stirs things up when students start dying. (978-1-60282-674-8)

Boys of Summer, edited by Steve Berman. Stories of young love and adventure, when the sky's ceiling is a bright blue marvel, when another boy's laughter at the beach can distract from dull summer jobs. (978-1-60282-663-2)

Street Dreams by Tama Wise. Tyson Rua has more than his fair share of problems growing up in New Zealand—he's gay, he's falling in love, and he's run afoul of the local hip-hop crew leader just as he's trying to make it as a graffiti artist. (978-1-60282-650-2)

me@you.com by KE Payne. Is it possible to fall in love with someone you've never met? Imogen Summers thinks so because it's happened to her. (978-1-60282-592-5)

Swimming to Chicago by David-Matthew Barnes. As the lives of the adults around them unravel, high school students Alex and

Robby form an unbreakable bond, vowing to do anything to stay together—even if it means leaving everything behind. (978-1-60282-572-7)

365 Days by KE Payne. Life sucks when you're seventeen years old and confused about your sexuality, and the girl of your dreams doesn't even know you exist. Then in walks sexy new emo girl, Hannah Harrison. Clemmie Atkins has exactly 365 days to discover herself, and she's going to have a blast doing it! (978-1-60282-540-6)

Timothy by Greg Herren. *Timothy* is a romantic suspense thriller from award-winning mystery writer Greg Herren set in the fabulous Hamptons. (978-1-60282-760-8)